LORI ADAMS

and the

RIVERBOAT MYSTERY

LORI ADAMS
and the
RIVERBOAT MYSTERY

by
Bernard Palmer

MOODY PRESS
CHICAGO

© 1971 by
THE MOODY BIBLE INSTITUTE
OF CHICAGO

ISBN 0-8024-4503-9

Eleventh Printing, 1982

Printed in the United States of America

Contents

CHAPTER   PAGE

1. A Strange Beginning   7
2. A Puzzling Rumor   18
3. Making Headlines   29
4. Off We Go!   40
5. The Search for the Margaret L   51
6. A Robbery   62
7. A Dangerous Encounter   73
8. Amazing Discoveries   83
9. Frustrated Hopes   95
10. Amos Jefferson's Clue   108
11. Something More than Gold   116

1

A Strange Beginning

It was a bright June morning when Cliff Adams turned off of the Interstate just beyond the bridge in Omaha. The sun had been up for hours and was peeking around the great fluffy clouds that marched in dazzling splendor across the pale blue sky. The breeze blew fitfully or not at all, teasing the murky, swirling water of the Missouri River and playing tag with the fresh green leaves that livened the trees. Mr. Adams negotiated the sharp curve, heading his new station wagon in the direction of the marina on the edge of the business district.

Lori Adams and her friend, Sharon Prentice, leaned forward on the front seat, trying to catch a glimpse of the river and the boats beyond the grimy buildings. Cliff slowed to a crawl, eyes searching for a sign or landmark that would indicate where to turn.

"Are you sure the man with the houseboat will be waiting for us, Dad?" Lori asked. She had been dreaming about the month on the river houseboat with her dad and Sharon for so long that it seemed like a fantasy, a dream that could never become reality. "Are you *sure* he wouldn't take somebody else?"

Cliff laughed good-naturedly. "If he's that kind of man I wouldn't want to charter his boat anyway."

"I don't think I've ever been on a houseboat before," Sharon observed.

Lori turned around in the seat to look at her best friend. "Neither have I. And to think, we may be spending all summer here!"

"I hope you're wrong about that," Cliff replied, slowing as they approached the marina. "I hope we get what we've come after long before the summer's half over."

Lori grinned up at him. She didn't mean that she really wanted to spend all summer aboard the *Betty Jo*. She knew her dad had a great deal of work to do and that this was only one project in a busy schedule at the museum. She was only trying to express her excitement at the prospect of being on the Missouri River houseboat for two or three weeks.

Lori was the first to spot the houseboat, a huge broad-beamed craft with a gleaming white superstructure.

"There she is, Dad!" she cried. "There she is!"

Sharon's eyes rounded in surprise. "I didn't think the boat would be so big or so beautiful."

"Neither did I."

"She's a beauty all right," Cliff said, pulling to a halt near the dock. "When we were corresponding about the charter, Captain Ellis wrote that the *Betty Jo* is almost new."

"Are we going aboard now?" Sharon asked.

"I don't see why not." He checked his watch. "Why don't you go aboard and tell Captain Ellis that I'll be along in about an hour? I've got some more gear to get and I want to check on our diver. He was supposed to have come in from New Orleans last night."

The girls got out of the car and watched Cliff drive away. Then they walked down to the water's edge. The marina was not large compared to those Lori had seen on the Mississippi River near their home, but it was filled to capacity with boats of every description. There were fishing boats and runabouts and cabin cruisers securely tied to the dock alongside sailboats and several houseboats.

At first the girls thought the marina was almost deserted. Now, however, they saw that there were a number of people around. Some were in their boats working. Others were busy on the dock or hurrying from their cars to their boats, arms loaded with supplies. No one was paying any attention to the two girls.

"I can hardly wait until your dad's diver gets here," Sharon said, her voice sounding louder in the comparative silence of the marina. "Won't it be exciting when he starts diving for that——"

Lori motioned her to silence quickly, before she could finish what she was saying.

"Be careful, Sharon," she warned in a hoarse whisper. "Remember what Dad said about not letting anyone know where we're going or what we're planning to do on this trip."

Fear shone in Sharon's pale green eyes and she caught her breath sharply. She looked about uneasily, trying to determine whether or not she had been overheard.

"Sorry! I forgot."

Lori wasn't sure why her dad had been insisting so strongly on secrecy about the expedition. It wasn't like him to be so concerned that no one know what he was about. In fact, the paper back home in Beechner usually carried complete accounts of the archeological trips Cliff made. He went along with it because the museum was largely supported by private donations and he thought it was good public relations to have people aware of what he was doing.

This trip, however, was different. He refused to give the paper any information about it. He even went so far as to ask them to print nothing about his being gone, saying that it was most important that there be no publicity.

This was something Lori had difficulty in understanding. She had heard him and Mother discuss the project at home. There were never any secrets in their house. What one member of the family knew they all knew. Lori couldn't see that there was anything different about the Missouri River project. Still, she knew her dad must have good reasons for his concern about publicity. He wouldn't do it if he didn't feel it was necessary.

Standing on the riverbank looking at the boats, Lori's thoughts went back to those last weeks in May. She was as excited as Sharon about the houseboat adventure they were going to be enjoying, but she came very close to missing the trip. She thought she would be spending the summer in Maine with her mother and Cindy and Jim.

At first Lori was as excited as Cindy and Jim were at the prospect of going to visit their cousins in Maine. Then she began thinking about her dad and the fact that he would be at home alone for the whole summer.

"Mother," she asked seriously, "can't Dad go along?"

"I wish he could, but he's got to stay at home and work."

The frown lines above Lori's eyes deepened. "He's going to get awfully lonesome."

That night when Mr. Adams came home, Lori met him at the car and walked up to the house talking to him. She told him what she had decided.

At first he didn't understand her. "Don't you *want* to go to Maine?"

"Oh, I want to go, all right," she replied quickly, "but I think I'll stay home and cook for you instead."

He bent and kissed her. "I couldn't ask you to do that, honey."

"But I don't want to go without you."

"We can talk about it later. OK?"

That answer didn't satisfy her, but she knew better than to press it. When Dad used that tone of voice the discussion was over and there was no use in trying to continue.

Lori tried to talk with her mother about staying home to keep Dad company, but for some reason she wasn't able to. That was the situation at the end of the week when her dad called her into the family room.

"You know, Lori, I've been thinking over that suggestion of yours about staying with me. Did you really mean it? Would you rather stay here than to go to Maine?"

"If you're going to be here alone, I would."

He tilted back in his easy chair. "Mother and I have been talking it over. We've decided that if you want to spend the summer with me, you can."

Her eyes brightened. She started to speak, but his lifted hand made her listen instead.

"There's something else I ought to tell you, Lori," he continued. "Actually, we won't be home, at least for the first part of the summer."

She looked up in surprise. "We won't?" she echoed. "Where will we be?"

"In a houseboat on the Missouri River."

Lori gasped. "What did you say?"

He laughed at her surprise. "We'll be in a houseboat on the river. Do you remember hearing me talk about the riverboat that was sunk on the Missouri over a hundred years ago?"

She nodded and waited for her dad to go on. The entire family had heard plenty about the stern-wheeled *Margaret L*, the heavily loaded riverboat that had been sunk on its way to Omaha. For the last six months Lori's father had been poring over old records and charts to learn more about it to figure out exactly where it went down. He believed that the boat still contained artifacts that would make it a real treasure for any archeologist or historian who was interested in the pioneer days.

But, most important was an old diary that was supposed to have been sealed in one of the first mason jars ever made. The diary belonged to Esau Carstigan, a scout for the Lewis and Clark expedition early in the nineteenth century. Then it became the property of Carstigan's daughter, Mrs. Sarah Miller, who left instructions in her will that it be sent to her daughter in Pennsylvania. It was that transfer that had placed the diary and the jar in the safe of the *Margaret L*, on the ill-fated trip.

There was a casual reference to the diary in the manifest, the record of the ship's cargo. Others had missed the mention of the book until Lori's dad discovered it and did enough research to reveal the significance of the Carstigan diary. Others had failed to link it to Lewis and Clark.

Mr. Adams appeared to be lost in thought and

Lori grew tired of waiting, so she asked, "Well, what about the *Margaret L?*"

Subconsciously he lowered his voice. "We're going to be looking for her, Lori."

"After all these years?"

He nodded. "A lot of people have tried to find it, without success, but I think I've discovered some records that pinpoint the place where it sank. At least I believe we can get close enough so we've got a reasonable chance of success."

"Wow! I can't wait!"

"I thought it would interest you."

Cliff didn't say anything about keeping the purpose of the trip a secret at first, even when she talked with him about inviting Sharon Prentice to go along. He even discussed the trip openly with her parents.

"We should allow ourselves a month to locate the *Margaret L* and raise her," he told Mr. and Mrs. Prentice. "But actually I have hopes of being able to do the job in less time than that."

The following week, however, Mr. Adams had a phone call that seemed to disturb him a great deal.

"What is it, Cliff?" Diane asked as he slowly returned the phone to its cradle. "Is there something wrong?"

He crossed the room slowly and turned. "That was the Nebraska Historical Society. They say there's a sudden surge of interest in the *Margaret L.*

They've had four requests for material about her in the last week."

"That isn't so serious, is it?"

"It could be. He said that there has been a revival of some of the old rumors about the actual cargo of the riverboat. They seem to be the basis of this new interest in her."

Diane eyed her husband questioningly. "What rumors?"

He glanced significantly at the girls and Jim, who were sitting on the floor listening. "We can talk about that later. OK?"

"What is it, Dad?" Lori asked.

He did not answer her question. "It's better if you don't know any more about it right now," he said, coming back and sitting down in his easy chair.

They thought he would change the subject, which was what he usually did when the conversation got on forbidden ground. But this time he didn't.

"There's something else that I want to warn you all about. Until now we've all talked openly about our summer project for the museum. This telephone call changes things. Don't say anything to anyone about what we will be doing. If anyone asks you about it, tell him he will have to talk to me."

They all nodded in agreement.

"I think we had better go over and talk to the Prentices, Diane," he continued, looking at his wife. "We'll have to see that they don't give the story of our trip any more publicity than it has had already."

The sudden switch to secrecy intrigued both Lori and Sharon. They talked about it often when they were alone together. It made the trip much more exciting than before.

"But I still can't figure out why it has to be such a big secret," Lori said. "Dad goes out on lots of projects like this one and most of the time the newspaper has stories about them."

Sharon Prentice shivered. "It makes me wonder who those people are who are trying to find the riverboat before we do and what they're looking for."

They were still wondering about it as they stood on the shore of the Missouri River at the Omaha marina and looked out across the murky water.

"We'd better get over to the houseboat and give Captain Ellis your dad's message."

"I guess we should." They started for the gleaming broad-beamed houseboat. "You know, Sharon, I don't believe there's anyone on board."

"Well," her friend retorted, "we'll never find out standing here."

They went out to the end of the dock and stepped onto the *Betty Jo*. The instant they did so, a rusty-colored shock of hair attached to a jeans-clad figure in tennis shoes popped out of the door.

"Can't you read? This is a private boat. No trespassing!"

The girls stopped abruptly, staring at the speaker in amazement. He was a boy about their own age; a long string bean of a boy with freckles and stormy blue eyes for a face.

"Didn't you hear me?" he repeated belligerently. "This is a private houseboat. So, just turn around and shove off."

Lori was too surprised to speak, but Sharon's temper flamed. "If you think you can scare us, you can think again. It so happens that Lori and I belong here."

He swaggered up to them. "Aw, come off it. You know better than that, so beat it."

"But it's true," Lori protested.

"Come on," Sharon said indignantly. "We were supposed to see the captain. We don't have time to visit with the boy who scrubs the deck."

The blue eyes almost popped out. "'The boy who scrubs the deck'!" he exploded. "I'll have you know that I'm as important as anyone aboard the *Betty Jo.* Now, are you going to get off our boat or do I have to help you?"

"You wouldn't dare!" Sharon said coldly, her fists clenching. "You wouldn't dare!"

2

A Puzzling Rumor

Lori spoke up quickly. "This is the *Betty Jo*, isn't it?"

The boy nodded. "What about it?"

"Then this is where we belong."

He gave the girls a disgusted look. "I've never seen such stupid females in my life. How many times do I have to tell you that we're chartered and the people are coming aboard this afternoon? Why don't you quit bugging me and just get out of here?"

Sharon glared at him. "We're just wasting our time with this—this individual," she retorted with contempt in her voice. "Come on, let's find Captain Ellis."

She started to push past the boy, who blocked their way, but at that instant a door behind him opened and a gaunt, red-haired man appeared.

"Hello there." His greeting was friendly.

"Hi."

"You must be the Adams girl."

"She certainly is," Sharon broke in. "And we would appreciate it if you would tell this—this *person* that we have a right to be on board."

Captain Ellis glanced at the boy who was obviously his son. "Rusty, these two girls are part of the party who have chartered the *Betty Jo*. I've been expecting them."

Rusty glared at them. "You've got to be kidding."

Captain Ellis acted as though he hadn't even heard his son. "I'm Capt. Arnold Ellis," he said, "but I guess you already know that. And this is my son, Gerald, who answers to the name of Rusty."

Sharon grimaced and Rusty scowled in return.

"I'm Lori Adams and this is my friend, Sharon Prentice."

"We're glad to know you." Captain Ellis extended a great, work-roughened hand. "Welcome aboard."

Rusty groaned audibly. "Two girls along for the whole trip! For crying out loud!"

"Don't pay any attention to him," Captain Ellis said, laughing. "He's allergic to girls."

Lori glanced at her companion. She wished Sharon and Rusty would get along better than they started out. They were going to be on the *Betty Jo* for several weeks together. And that was a long time to be with someone you didn't like. She was thinking about Sharon and Rusty when her friend broke in on her thoughts.

"Aren't you going to tell Captain Ellis what your dad said?"

"That's right. I completely forgot it." She turned to the tall skipper of the houseboat. "Dad sent us

ahead to tell you that he has some things to attend to
in town. He'll be along as soon as he can."

"Fine. Fine. Rusty and I have everything ship-
shape. By the time your dad gets here we'll be ready
to shove off. You'll be wanting to see your quarters
for the next few weeks."

He took them into the houseboat and showed
them a large, clean, attractive stateroom on the side
facing the dock. There were twin beds along the
inside bulkhead, two easy chairs, and a writing desk.
In the opposite corner there was a small television.

The girls slowly looked around the big room,
surveying it with approval.

"Why, it's beautiful!" Lori exclaimed.

"I thought you'd like it." Captain Ellis excused
himself. "I've got some last minute things to do,
myself. If you want anything, just ask Rusty or me.
We want you to be comfortable while you're
aboard."

Lori thanked him and closed the door behind him.
Sharon was already sprawling comfortably in one of
the chairs, watching television.

"Isn't this terrific?" Lori asked. "It's as nice as my
room at home."

Sharon shrugged. "It would be if it wasn't for that
conceited Rusty Ellis."

"I thought you liked him," Lori teased.

"Me?" Contempt filled her voice. "I can't stand
him!"

"He's not as bad as all that, is he?"

"As a matter of fact, he's worse!"

The two girls remained in their stateroom until Cliff Adams came aboard. They heard his voice on deck and went out to meet him. Rusty and the captain were already there, talking to Cliff.

"It's OK with me if you don't want to leave this afternoon," Captain Ellis was saying. "Most of the guests who charter us want to get out on the river as soon as possible. That's what we've been preparing for."

"*We're* as anxious to get out there as anyone, but we're going to have to delay our departure for a day or two."

"I see." But his expression showed just the opposite. "We can take a couple of short shakedown cruises while we're waiting, if that's all right with you."

"Sounds OK to me. It'll give us something to do."

"And," the captain added, "we'll have a chance to get acquainted."

Rusty scowled. "We're already acquainted," he said rudely.

Sharon wrinkled her nose at him expressively.

When Lori and Sharon were alone with Cliff in his stateroom they asked him about the delay.

"We thought you wanted to get out of here as quickly as possible," his daughter said.

"I do. But our diver is working at one of the offshore oil rigs right now. An emergency has come up and he wasn't able to get away as soon as he thought he could. He won't be able to make it here until day after tomorrow." He shrugged his shoulders. "So, there's nothing for us to do except wait."

They went out on deck presently and Captain Ellis joined them, noting the time. "Dinner will be served in an hour," he said. "And I almost forgot to tell you. Rusty is the cook on the *Betty Jo*."

Sharon wrinkled her nose distastefully.

"He's really a good cook. I taught him myself after his mother died."

"The girls can help him," Cliff said, volunteering their services.

"I'm sure he would much rather cook and do the dishes alone than have us get in the way," Lori replied quickly.

"Guess again," Rusty retorted. "I think that's the best suggestion I've heard since you two came aboard. Now, if you'll come into the galley with me, I'll start breaking you in."

Before the girls could protest he started for the galley. There was little they could do except follow him.

"It was real thoughtful of you to volunteer to cook while we're out. You don't know how much I appreciate it."

"Don't get so excited about it," Sharon said icily. "You know as well as we do that we got roped into it."

"How you talk!"

Lori and Sharon were surprised to see how

capable Rusty actually was in the galley. He set to work methodically, preparing the evening meal. It wasn't just the matter of opening a few cans and setting a loaf of bread on the table. He fried chicken, prepared mashed potatoes and gravy, and fixed a salad and two vegetables.

"How did you learn to cook so well?" Lori asked him.

"Didn't you hear what Dad said? He taught me. And I've been doing the cooking aboard the *Betty Jo* ever since."

He put water on for the dishes to soak and turned to Sharon. "I guess we're ready to eat. You can call them to dinner now."

She acted as though she was about to refuse but changed her mind and went to get them.

Captain Ellis and Rusty would have started eating as soon as everyone was seated at the table but Cliff suggested that they return thanks first. The suggestion seemed to embarrass the captain of the houseboat.

"I guess we can ask a prayer for the food, if you want to," he said reluctantly. "It's your charter. You're entitled to do as you please."

"Thank you." Cliff paused until they had all bowed their heads. Then he prayed briefly, asking God's blessing on the food. When he finished and looked up he couldn't help noticing that Captain Ellis' face was flushed.

"Is there something wrong?"

The skipper shook his head quickly. "Oh, no. There's nothing wrong. Nothing at all. I was just thinking about my wife. She was a real religious person. She was the last one who ever prayed on a boat of mine, and that was more than three years ago."

After a time the conversation drifted to the sunken riverboat Cliff had come to Omaha to look for. "I've heard a lot of scuttlebutt about the old *Margaret L* along the river in my day, but I never thought I'd ever be involved in hunting for her," Captain Ellis observed.

"To tell you the truth I didn't think I would be interested in trying to find her either. But she'll be a real historical find if we can locate and raise her. According to the manifest she was loaded to the gunnels."

The captain's eyes narrowed. "That she was. I'd bet my last dollar on that fact."

Rusty had stopped eating and was studying Cliff's face intently. "From what I hear," the boy broke in, "she was carrying some cargo that wasn't on the manifest."

His father's gaze narrowed, warning him to silence. But he chose to ignore it.

"She was carrying gold!" he whispered mysteriously. "A million dollars' worth!"

Lori and Sharon both gasped. A million dollars' worth of gold! No wonder other people were trying to beat them to the *Margaret L*!

Cliff's expression did not change. "You don't really believe that, do you, Rusty?"

"You bet I do," the boy replied. "The man who told me heard it from his great-grandfather who was one of the crew who managed to get away after she sank."

"There's always a lot of wild talk," Captain Ellis put in, glaring at his son in an effort to silence him. "You can't always believe everything you hear."

"You heard him too, Dad, less than a week ago," Rusty exploded. "He was sitting right where Lori is, telling us about his great-grandfather and all the gold. It had to be true. He even helped load it! And he was almost scalped by the Indians who sank the old stern-wheeler."

"I've heard that same story and a couple of variations of it," Cliff continued patiently. "One was that a band of renegade Indians had gotten a small cannon by ambushing a detachment of soldiers and managed to fire it, hitting the *Margaret L* and sinking her so fast there wasn't time to take the gold off before she went down. Neat trick, if you ask me."

"That's almost the same story we heard," Captain Ellis put in.

"The other story is that three or four army deserters stole the cannon from Fort Omaha, dressed up like Indians, and used the cannon to sink the riverboat."

Captain Ellis spooned sugar into his coffee. "I never heard of Indians firing a cannon," he said.

"Neither have I and I've done quite a lot of research on the subject. That's the reason I've put more stock in the story of the deserters."

"What difference does it make who it was?" Rusty wanted to know. "The boat was sunk and that's the main thing."

"You're right about that, only I haven't told the rest of the story," Cliff continued. "The ones who sank the *Margaret L* located the wreckage, dove down to her, and got the gold for themselves."

"It makes sense to me," Captain Ellis admitted. "I can't imagine a million dollars in gold lying around, unfound, for a hundred years."

"You just wait and see, Dad," Rusty said. "If we locate the old riverboat, you'll find out the gold is still aboard." He directed his attention to Cliff. "And I'll tell you another thing. You don't fool me. You're not here to try and find *historical artifacts* that are on the old boat. You're here to find that gold, like everybody else."

"Rusty!" The boy's nickname exploded from his dad's lips. "We've had all the talk about gold and the purpose of Mr. Adams' search that we're going to have. Do you understand?"

The boy fell silent but his face expressed his disbelief.

Cliff tried to talk about other things but the spontaneity had gone out of the conversation. No one at the table seemed interested in visiting. As soon as Lori and Sharon had helped Rusty with the dishes, they excused themselves and went into their cabin.

"Did you hear what Rusty said about the gold that is supposed to be on the sunken riverboat?" Sharon whispered as soon as they were alone.

Lori nodded.

"Do you believe it's still there?"

"Dad doesn't think it's there and he's done a lot of studying about the *Margaret L.* I'm sure he'd know if there was a chance that there was anything like that aboard."

"Maybe that's the reason he's been so anxious to keep our trip a secret, Lori," her friend persisted. "Maybe the man who called him from the Nebraska Historical Society told him that the million dollars in gold is really on the sunken riverboat and that's why he wants to keep it a secret."

"No," Lori replied firmly. "If Dad says he doesn't believe that gold is on board then he doesn't believe it. He's telling the truth!"

"*Anybody* would lie about a million dollars," Sharon said. "I don't blame him."

"Not Dad. He wouldn't lie, because he's a Christian."

Sharon stared at her, questions going through her mind but remaining unasked. "There you go with that Christian stuff again," she retorted. "I don't get it."

Lori drew a deep breath. Sharon had been her very best friend for as long as she could remember.

They went to the same school and used to go to the same Sunday school and church. But when Lori and Cindy and Jim decided to let Jesus have full control of their lives, things hadn't been the same with Sharon.

Lori still walked to school with her and did homework with her, and if anybody asked, she was always quick to say that Sharon was her best friend. But there were times when it seemed to Lori that she didn't really know Sharon at all.

Lori paused, trying to find words to explain to Sharon why her dad would not lie, if he thought there was gold on the boat they were looking for. Before she could answer, Sharon closed the subject decisively.

"Well, I can tell you one thing. Rusty doesn't believe that your dad is telling the truth about the gold and the *Margaret L.* And I'm not sure that Captain Ellis does either."

"That doesn't make any difference," Lori answered. "When we find the riverboat and get her raised, everybody will see that Dad wasn't being dishonest."

"Oh sure. *Sure*," her friend replied, doubt evident in her voice.

3

Making Headlines

When they went into the galley for breakfast the following morning, Lori expected Rusty to start talking about the gold again. But he did not. Instead he acted agreeable, as though nothing had happened. Mr. Adams was pleasant enough himself that morning, but he seemed preoccupied. Shortly after breakfast he said that he had to be gone for a while.

"I've got quite a lot to do," he told them. "The chances are that I won't be back until the middle of the afternoon."

Captain Ellis nodded. "What do you want me to do about that shakedown trip, Cliff? Should we wait until you get back?"

He shook his head. "The girls will enjoy it. Go right ahead."

"Maybe we'll do that."

Lori eyed him quizzically. She wasn't sure, but there seemed to be something strange about the captain, something she couldn't quite figure out. She was still thinking about it when her dad kissed her good-bye, turned, and sprang onto the dock.

"I'll see you when I get back."

Captain Ellis waved to him indifferently. After the station wagon pulled away he turned to his son. "I'll start the engines, Rusty. Get ready to cast off."

"Sure thing."

Lori was watching with some amusement. "I thought you were always supposed to say, 'Aye aye, sir,' when you're given an order."

Rusty grinned with amusement. "That's only in books," he said. "On Missouri River houseboats we always say, 'sure thing.' "

"I'm glad to know that."

"I'll bet." He loosed the heavy line aft and moved to the bow.

The heavy houseboat moved away from the dock and out into the river, inching its way to the main channel. Captain Ellis reversed the engines and brought the boat to a stop, holding it motionless with the twin screws, while a tug pulling half a dozen barges glided past. When the way was clear he got under way again.

The houseboat moved slowly with a certain dignity, as though the *Betty Jo* was different from the average riverboat. And that it was. It was bigger than most of the pleasure craft on that part of the Missouri, for one thing, and more luxuriously appointed. It was a castle compared to most of the boats berthed at the marina.

When they were under way Rusty came over to the side rail by Sharon and Lori.

"Isn't this exciting?" Sharon asked, for once speaking to him without losing her temper.

He grinned. "I don't know whether I'd call it exciting or not. It's pretty old stuff to me. You see Dad and I spend an awful lot of time on the river."

Lori leaned on the railing and looked out toward the city. Sharon was right about the houseboat being exciting. It was thrilling just to be on board and watch the other boats. It would be even more exciting when they started looking for the sunken *Margaret L.*

After a brief moment Rusty turned to Lori. "It must be exciting for you to have your dad go out on a project like this."

"It is," she replied cryptically.

She did not look directly at him but she had the uncomfortable feeling that he was studying her intently. He continued. "What did you say your dad does?"

"I didn't say, but he's the curator of the museum at Beechner, Iowa, where we live."

His eyes narrowed. "He told me that he's an archeologist." There was accusation in his voice, as though he had just caught her dad in a lie.

"Oh, he's an archeologist too," she said quickly. "That's what he calls himself when anyone asks him about his work. But he's also the curator of the museum."

Lori couldn't tell whether he believed her or not.

"I suppose that could be," he acknowledged, "but

it's not the reason he's looking for that old riverboat,
is it?"

"It certainly is." Indignation crept into her young
voice. "And for your information, it's the *only*
reason that he's searching for the *Margaret L.*
He doesn't believe that story about the million
dollars in gold that's supposed to be aboard."

Rusty was breathing hard. "Oh now, come off it.
You don't expect us to believe that, do you?"

"It happens to be the truth."

"You might fool my dad, but you don't fool me,"
he continued irritably. "Every once in a while some
guys get a wild idea about looking for that old boat.
And they've always got some good-sounding reason
for wanting it. Some reason besides the gold. But
they don't fool anyone."

Lori could feel her cheeks get warm. She could
also feel Sharon smirking triumphantly, as though
Rusty's questioning proved her own opinion.

"You might not believe it now, but when we raise
the riverboat and you see that there's no gold aboard
her, you'll know that Dad's telling you the truth."

They dropped the subject and enjoyed the ride
for a few minutes. When Rusty finally spoke again, it
was in a different mood. You and your dad don't
have to worry about us telling anybody anything.
We'll keep your secret. We won't tell anyone that
you're actually looking for the *Margaret L* gold."

"But we're *not!*" Lori cried in desperation. "You
won't believe anything either of us tells you, but it's

the truth. The only thing Dad is interested in is the historical items that are on board, especially an old diary. I can't tell you any more than that."

Disbelief edged his laughter. "All right. Have it your way. But just remember this: We all know that you're lying."

With that he swaggered away.

Sharon said nothing about the exchange but Lori knew that she agreed with Rusty. She had told her as much the night before.

Captain Ellis returned to the dock about one o'clock, filled the fuel tanks once more, and waited for Lori's dad. Cliff returned to the marina shortly before three o'clock, new concern carved into his usually happy features.

"Is everything set, Dad?" Lori wanted to know.

"I got the gear we need," he told her, "but I called McMillan, the diver we've hired. He's still working on that oil job and doesn't know if he'll be able to finish by tomorrow night."

Lori was trying to decide whether to tell him about her conversation with Rusty when Captain Ellis approached them.

"There's someone here to see you," Captain Ellis told him.

A slight, pleasant-faced individual came aboard and introduced himself. "I'm John Hamer, a reporter for the *Omaha Register.*"

Cliff stiffened slightly. Lori saw the suspicion in his eyes. He didn't want to talk to a reporter right then, she was sure of that. Yet he was cordial and invited the stranger into his stateroom. She followed along.

"I understand that you're planning on making a search for the riverboat the *Margaret L*," Mr. Hamer began.

Cliff started to answer him, but stopped suddenly and turned to his daughter. "Lori, honey, would you go and tell Captain Ellis that I'll be busy for a time?"

"He knows that, I think," she said, hoping that was enough to satisfy him.

"I know that, but I'd like to have you go and tell him anyway."

Reluctantly she left the stateroom. He closed the door behind her harder than necessary. That was a surprising development. Why would he agree to talk with the reporter? And why would he insist that she leave, and then shut the door behind her?

Sharon was waiting outside the captain's quarters when she came out.

"How do you suppose a reporter found out about your dad's project?" she whispered.

Lori shook her head. That was only one of the things that was troubling her.

"Rusty could have let it slip somewhere," her friend continued.

"I suppose he could have," Lori agreed. Actually, she hoped that he hadn't. "But there are other ways a reporter could have gotten wind of the story. Someone could have overheard us talking, or

someone might have learned of the supplies Dad has
been buying and guessed at the reason for it, or Mr.
Hamer may have some connections in Beechner. He
might have heard the story from there. At first we
didn't make any effort to hide anything."

Mr. Hamer was in the stateroom with Lori's dad
for an hour before coming out on deck, his cartridge
tape recorder in his hand.

"Thank you, Mr. Adams. I appreciate the material
you've given me." With that, he stepped off onto the
dock.

Captain Ellis was surprised that Cliff had talked
with the reporter and said so. "After all, I thought
you were anxious to keep the real purpose for this
trip as quiet as possible."

"I am," Cliff said, "and if I'd done what I wanted
to I wouldn't have talked with John Hamer, but I
figured that I had to give him some information or
he'd get his story from other sources and do us more
harm than ever."

The captain frowned. "You may be right, Cliff,
but I'm not sure I would have run the risk if I were
you."

Lori saw that her dad's shoulders seemed to sag
heavily. She wanted to talk to him about it, but she
decided not to. He would tell her on his own if he
thought she should know something.

The visit of the newspaper reporter seemed to
cover the houseboat with gloom that night. Dinner
the evening before had been fun. They all sat around

the table for almost an hour after they finished eating, going over their plans for the next few days and talking about the *Margaret L* and her cargo. Tonight, they spoke very little. Cliff was particularly preoccupied. He cut his meat and ate mechanically, a faraway look in his eyes. He answered if someone asked him a question or spoke directly to him, but that was all. He scarcely seemed to notice when the girls excused themselves and left the table.

"What's wrong tonight?" Sharon asked in a low voice as she and Lori stood together at the railing of the houseboat. "Your dad acts like the world just fell in."

"I was thinking about that myself," Lori told her. "The only thing I can think of is that he's upset about that reporter's visit. Didn't you see how disturbed he was when John Hamer left the *Betty Jo?*"

Sharon didn't answer right away. She sat watching the moonlight shimmer on the water. "There are a lot of things about this trip that bother me."

Lori glanced quickly at her friend. "What makes you say that?"

A smile rested briefly on Sharon's lips before she could stop it. "Skip it," she said, shrugging her indifference. "I was just thinking."

Lori's expression changed. Although Sharon hadn't put it into words, she knew well enough what her friend was hinting at. She still believed that Cliff was actually searching for the sunken riverboat because of the gold bullion that was supposed to be aboard. Like Rusty, she thought the talk about the diary was just a dodge.

What bothered Lori even worse was that Sharon hadn't believed her when she protested that her dad was a Christian and wouldn't lie. As far as Sharon was concerned, she didn't believe that a Christian was any different from anyone else when it came to telling the truth about a million dollars in gold.

Lori stared at her questioningly. What could she say that would make Sharon believe her and her dad? What could she tell Sharon that would prove to her that she was wrong?

Sharon asked if she'd like to play checkers, but Lori didn't respond. So Sharon wrote to her mother while Lori walked around the deck. Finally, they went into their stateroom and went to bed.

When breakfast was over the following day Cliff took a dime from his pocket and handed it to Lori. "Would you girls run up to the drugstore and get a morning paper for me?"

"You don't expect that story to be out so soon, do you?" Captain Ellis asked.

Cliff looked up. "I suppose not. But if it does come out, I don't want to miss it. I've got to see how much trouble it's apt to cause us."

The girls left the houseboat and made their way up the narrow road to the business district.

"I wish we could get on our way," Sharon said,

looking furtively about. "I keep thinking that somebody is going to try to stop us."

Lori pulled in a deep breath. She was uneasy too, but she didn't dare allow herself to think about it. "We can't leave until our diver gets here."

"That's another thing that bothers me. You don't suppose someone is deliberately keeping the diver away, do you?"

"Why would they do that?"

"To keep us from going after the riverboat, of course."

Lori shuddered. That was something she hadn't thought about. It didn't seem likely that a diver from New Orleans could be kept from going to Omaha, but if the right people believed there was gold aboard the *Margaret L* and wanted to stop her dad, it was entirely possible.

They got the morning paper, but Mr. Hamer's story wasn't in it. Cliff went over it hurriedly. "I guess it was a little on the quick side to expect it to be in the morning edition when he only took the interview yesterday afternoon."

"Maybe it won't be printed at all," Lori said hopefully.

"That's too much to expect." He sighed deeply. "It'll be printed sooner or later. I'm convinced of that."

When the girls bought a copy of the afternoon paper the story was on the front page.

"Look!" Lori cried, dismay edging her voice.

Sharon read the headlines aloud. "New Search
For Army Gold?"

"Oh, Sharon! That's terrible!"

They paid for the paper and hurried out of the
store.

"Rusty and I aren't the only ones who don't buy
that story about looking for somebody's old diary."

But Lori wasn't listening. Things couldn't be
worse! Every crackpot in the country would be sure
that Mr. Adams and the others were looking for the
riverboat in order to find the gold.

Cliff's face turned pale as he took the paper from
his daughter and read the headline.

"Oh, no!" He wrinkled one side in an angry grip.

"About what I expected," Captain Ellis said
cryptically. "He had to make it as sensational as he
could."

Cliff read the story hurriedly. "I might have
known it!"

4
Off We Go!

Cliff Adams went into his stateroom, the afternoon paper still in his hand, and closed the door behind him. He was not the only one who read the *Omaha Register's* account of his coming search for the sunken riverboat. He had scarcely finished reading the story when two men came aboard the *Betty Jo* and asked for him.

Captain Ellis surveyed the pair suspiciously. The spokesman was shorter than he was by at least half a head, and even in his gray business suit, he was rough-looking. His companion was short also, but he was just the opposite to the other in appearance. His shaggy blond hair needed to be cut and he wore a beat-up denim jacket. The spokesman stood with his feet planted firmly and his hands on his waist inside his coat. The second man kept changing his position and looking around nervously.

"We want to see Cliff Adams," the spokesman said. "Where is he?"

The skipper's expression didn't change. "That depends on a couple of things. Does he know you? And does he want to talk to you?"

"Maybe he does and maybe he doesn't," the short stranger replied. "What business is that of yours?"

"Anything that goes on aboard this boat is my business, friend," he said sternly. "Just remember that."

The spokesman smiled condescendingly. "There's no need for you to get your back up. We'd just like to visit with Cliff for a little while. My name's Buford Kelly and this is Tim Nickerson."

"I see." Captain Ellis smiled insincerely at them. "If you want to wait a minute I'll go see if he wants to talk to you."

"Maybe you'd better let us do our own talking," Nickerson said.

"Tim!" Kelly snapped at his nervous companion. "That'll be fine, captain. We'll wait out here on deck."

Lori and Sharon could see the two strangers from their vantage point inside their stateroom.

"What do you suppose those men want?" Sharon whispered, although the visitors were out of earshot.

Lori breathed deeply. She hadn't been able to hear any of the conversation but they must have come because of the article in the paper, she reasoned. "I don't know for sure, but it must have something to do with the *Margaret L.*"

"I don't like the looks of them."

"Neither do I." Lori half hoped that her dad would not talk to the strangers, but a moment or so later he came out on deck and shook hands with them.

"Maybe he knows them," Sharon observed.

"That couldn't be," Lori replied.

On deck they saw Captain Ellis introduce Cliff to the two men.

"Is there someplace where we can talk?" Buford Kelly asked.

"I guess so. We can go over there and sit down." He gestured toward a cluster of chairs on the foredeck.

"No," Kelly said, shaking his head. "We want to talk to you in private."

"I don't think that is necessary for anything we have to say to each other," Cliff said coldly, "but if you wish, we can go into my stateroom."

Kelly smiled. "That would be much better."

Lori and Sharon watched as her dad took the two men into his quarters and closed the door.

"I'd like to know what that's all about," Sharon whispered tensely.

Lori nodded. "Come on. Let's go outside where we can see something."

On deck Rusty met them. "Who are those characters?"

"I never saw them before in my life," Lori said.

"They're not here to see about finding *historical artifacts*," he said significantly. "I can tell you *that* much right now."

She blushed and turned away. Like Sharon, Rusty had already made up his mind as to the purpose of the trip and it wouldn't do any good to protest.

He turned to Lori and his mouth opened as though he was about to speak. Instead he turned abruptly and went into the wheelhouse where his dad was sitting.

The two girls cautiously made their way along the houseboat railing until they were even with Cliff's stateroom. But they could see nothing; the heavy drapes were tightly drawn.

"It's no use," Sharon said disappointedly, "we can't see a thing."

"And we can't hear anything from out here either."

They looked at each other, both girls thinking, what are we going to do now?

They went back to the bow just in time to see the door open and Lori's dad and his two visitors appear on deck. As far as Kelly and Nickerson were concerned the interview must not have gone too well. They were both scowling.

"You'd better think over our proposition, Adams," Buford Kelly was saying. "You haven't got a chance of finding the *Margaret L* unless you play along with us."

"I appreciate your concern for me but that's a risk I have to take." They didn't miss the sarcasm in his voice.

"You'll be sorry," Nickerson warned.

Cliff did not reply.

The two men left the boat and were halfway to

their car before Kelly turned back. "You're sure you won't change your mind?"

"I'm positive."

"A million dollars is a big enough haul for all of us."

"There's no use in my talking to you any longer," Cliff told them. "I've already explained that I'm not after gold bullion. I don't even believe there is any aboard the riverboat. As you read in the paper and I told you just now, I'm after valuable historical items for my museum. Period."

Nickerson wanted to stay and argue, but his companion grasped his arm. "Come on, Tim. He won't pay any attention to us. So, we're on our own!"

As soon as their car pulled away, Captain Ellis came out on deck. "Your friends didn't seem too happy with you when they left."

The corners of Cliff's mouth tightened. "I don't like this, captain. I think we'd better get under way immediately."

"What about your diver? I thought you said you had to wait for him."

"I can come back to pick him up," he answered. "Or we can leave word for him to rent a car and come down to where we'll be working. There's some preliminary work that we can get out of the way."

The captain scratched his head thoughtfully. "I think you've got a point, but there's some paper work I ought to do before we leave the marina. I don't think I can get it finished in time to leave before dark."

Cliff drew himself erect. "But you can do it tomorrow, can't you?"

"Yes. I suppose," the skipper said.

"Then I think that's what we'd better do." He lowered his voice to a whisper. "To tell you the truth, captain, I didn't like the looks of those two. I don't trust them."

"Neither do I." He checked his watch. "I think we can be ready to leave tonight if we get to work. I'll just check the fuel and make up a grocery list. We can be ready to leave in an hour."

"Good. That'll give me time enough to go over my gear again and see that I've got everything."

Sharon and Lori didn't know that they were planning to leave the marina that night until Captain Ellis knocked on their door and asked them to take a grocery list to the supermarket in town.

"If you tell them that we're in a hurry," he said, "they'll bring it right over. In fact, they'll probably give you a ride back to the marina in their truck."

The girls left the *Betty Jo* and walked briskly up the street. "I can't understand it at all," Sharon said uneasily. "The last we heard, they didn't plan to go out for several days. Now we're supposed to get under way in an hour."

Lori nodded. "I think those two men had something to do with it. Both Dad and Captain Ellis acted like they just made up their minds to leave tonight."

They stopped for a red light.

"I wish we were already on the river. That's what I wish."

Before Lori could answer, she spied a car being parked across the street. There was something about this one that attracted her attention. It was a new green convertible with a license plate so muddy it could not be read. There was a diagonal crack in the front window on the driver's side.

"Sharon," she whispered, with fright in her voice. "Does that car look familiar?"

"The car that belongs to those two men who came to see your dad had a cracked window like that, and it was a green convertible."

Lori caught her breath sharply, unaware that her fingers were digging into her friend's arm. "It's *got* to be them."

At that moment the girls realized that the two men in the car had seen them.

"And they're watching us!" The color fled from Sharon's cheeks.

Before the girls could decide what to do, the driver's door opened and Buford Kelly got out.

"What are we going to do?" Sharon demanded, her voice shaking.

"They're coming this way! Let's get out of here!"

Whirling, the girls raced back down the street toward the marina. They dodged past a woman who had been a few feet behind them. almost ran into two men walking out of an alley, and kept going. Their hearts were pounding so hard it hurt but they did not slow down.

They heard the car door slam, followed by the starting of the engine and the squeal of tires on the pavement as the convertible peeled out of its parking place. Sharon and Lori dashed across the highway and down the narrow street to the marina. They did not stop until they were safely aboard the houseboat once more.

Captain Ellis heard them clamber on deck and came out of the wheel house quickly.

"What's the matter?" he demanded.

"Those two men!" Sharon exclaimed between gasps. "We saw them!"

His eyes narrowed. "And you got all excited and upset about that?"

"They were coming after us!" Lori added.

The tall captain looked straight into Lori's eyes. "Are you sure about that?"

"Positive."

"You girls had better go inside. I'll send Rusty after the groceries."

"At first I didn't think he was going to believe us," Sharon said when they were alone.

"But he did."

A moment or two later Rusty came out of the wheelhouse, pushed past them, and stepped onto the dock. His dad must have warned him to be careful, Lori decided. He took a couple of steps,

then stopped and looked around before advancing
again. When he seemed satisfied that the two men
were nowhere in sight, he left the dock and strode
confidently up the street.

"I think we ought to go tell Dad what happened,"
Lori suggested.

"Good idea."

They knocked lightly on his stateroom door, but
there was no answer.

"Maybe he isn't in there," Sharon said.

"He has to be. Captain Ellis didn't tell us he went
anywhere." She tried the door, surprised to find that
it was locked. "Dad!" she called. "Dad!" Still no
answer.

"He's not in," Sharon repeated. "If he was, he'd
answer you."

"Dad!" Lori pounded the door.

They were about to turn away when he called out.
"Just a minute, Lori. I'll be right with you."

She tried the door again, as though she could not
quite believe that he would lock his door to keep
them out. He hadn't locked the door at any other
time on the boat. In fact, she couldn't remember
that he had ever locked his study door at home,
whether he was there or not. This was a strange
development.

There was a metallic click on the other side of the
door and Mr. Adams appeared. "Come on in," he
said, smiling.

Lori saw that his desk was cleared off. The books

were pushed back and the clock was moved to the far edge. They could tell that he had had something on it moments before, something he wanted to put away before he let them into his stateroom.

"Well, what's on your minds?" He was trying hard to be relaxed and cheerful. A little too hard, Lori felt.

They told him what had taken place. He nodded approvingly as they related how they had turned and run. "I'm glad you did," he broke in. "I don't ever want you to take any risks, and especially not with men like Kelly and Nickerson."

"You don't have to worry about that," Sharon said. "At least as far as I'm concerned. We took one look at those two and decided that we didn't want to tangle with them."

Cliff went over to the divan and sat down heavily. "Of course, we've got to realize that it might have been a coincidence, your seeing them there."

"Yes it might be at that," Lori said. "But I don't think so. Mr. Kelly got out of the car as soon as he saw us, didn't he, Sharon?"

Her girl friend nodded vigorously. "And the other one—Nickerson—got out too. They were after us, all right."

"But it was in broad daylight," Cliff countered. "That's what seems so strange to me. I can't think they would dare to attempt to grab you girls out in public and in the daytime. They ought to know they couldn't get away with anything like that."

Since neither girl had considered that aspect, they didn't know what to say for a minute.

"It may seem strange to you," Sharon retorted finally, "but it's the truth. They were after us, weren't they, Lori?"

Cliff got to his feet. "Did you stop to think that they may only have wanted to talk to you?" he asked. "That's a possibility too, you know."

"Maybe it is but they sure had a funny way of going about it."

He pulled in a deep breath and exhaled the air slowly.

"Regardless of what those fellows had in mind just now, I think it's a good idea to get out of here as quick as we can. After all the publicity we've had, the chances are that other crackpots will be snooping around, too."

In spite of their haste it was dark before Captain Ellis said they could leave. He started the engines and the *Betty Jo* moved slowly away from the dock.

"Well," Lori said to no one in particular, "we're on our way."

"That's right," Rusty answered. "We're on our way to find that million dollars in gold bullion." He stopped deliberately and faced her, a teasing look on his freckled features. "Oh! I beg your *pardon*!" He mimicked Lori. "It isn't gold bullion we're after. It's *historical artifacts*!"

Rusty's mocking laughter drifted across the still night air.

5

The Search for the Margaret L

There had been so much excitement since the story appeared in the *Omaha Register* that Lori and Sharon had almost forgotten the trip they would be making aboard the *Betty Jo*. However, as the houseboat glided majestically down the broad river, they went out on deck and leaned on the railing. All was silent except for the muffled throb of the engines.

"Aren't the lights of the city beautiful?" Sharon said softly.

"I was just thinking the same thing. It's so beautiful and so peaceful that it's hard to believe there are people like that awful Buford Kelly and Tim Nickerson in the world."

"Why did you have to bring that up?" Sharon asked. "I was just beginning to enjoy myself."

The houseboat met a tug pulling a string of oil barges upstream. The girls went over to the starboard bow and watched until the barges were behind them. They had not moved when Lori's dad approached.

"I was wondering where you girls were," he said.

"You didn't think we had gone anywhere, did you?" Lori asked, laughing good-naturedly.

"I was just thinking that it was about time you did go somewhere." He looked at his watch. "You'd better turn in now, girls. Unless I'm badly mistaken, we're going to have a long, hard day tomorrow."

They went back to their stateroom presently and Lori took her Bible from the dresser.

"Are you going to read that again?" Sharon asked her.

"Like I told you, I always read the Bible at night before I go to bed."

Sharon sat down on her bunk and took off her tennis shoes. "Lori, will you level with me on something?"

"Of course I will."

"You don't *really* believe that your dad is looking for an old diary on the *Margaret L*, do you?"

Lori's gaze met hers. "Yes," she said simply. "I do."

"You're the only one who does."

"That might be, but I still believe him. He wouldn't tell us that if it wasn't true."

Sharon slipped into her pajamas but put on her housecoat instead of going to bed. "What makes you so sure?"

"The Bible tells us that we're not supposed to lie, and Dad's a Christian," she explained. "That's why I'm so sure."

"I don't think he's doing something *bad*. He's just telling it to people who don't have any business knowing what his real plans are."

Lori thought about that. She knew that a lot of kids and grownups, too, had the idea that there are different kinds of lies, and some are worse than others. There were outright lies and white lies and half-truths and all sorts of classifications of falsehoods.

But even before they became Christians, Dad and Mother had taught them that all lying was wrong. It didn't make any difference what reason was behind the lie. Now that they were followers of Jesus Christ, their folks stressed truth-telling more than ever.

"Yes, he would be doing something *very* bad," Lori countered. "The Bible tells us that we shouldn't lie. It doesn't say anything about 'white' lies or having a good reason for telling things that aren't true."

Sharon turned that over in her mind. "I tell things that aren't really true sometimes," she admitted. "But only if it's about something that's nobody else's business or if it's something that won't hurt anybody. And so do my folks. Like if somebody calls for Dad and he doesn't want to have to go back to the office that night, he'll have Mother tell them that he's not home. There isn't anything wrong with that, is there?"

Lori pulled in a deep breath.

"Dad always says that God set down the 'ab-

solutes' that we're to live by. We're not supposed to
cheat or steal or lie. We're not supposed to want
things that belong to other people or to be jealous
when good things happen to them. He says that it
doesn't make any difference what we think or would
like to believe. God's Word is the final authority."

"So?"

"So, any kind of lying or cheating or dishonesty is
sin. It doesn't make any difference whether lies are
big or little, important or unimportant. There are no
excuses for them."

Sharon eyed her thoughtfully. "I've never heard
anything like that before. I don't think I could do it."

"I don't think you could either."

At that Sharon bristled slightly. She hadn't expected such a statement from her friend. "What do
you mean?"

"None of us can live the sort of lives we ought to
live," Lori continued. "I can't and neither could you
or anyone else. But God knew that from the
beginning so He prepared a way for us to live good
lives. Jesus Christ will help you to live the way you
should, just as He helps me and Dad and Mother
and anyone else who confesses his sin and puts his
trust in Jesus."

"How do I do that?" Sharon asked.

"Tell God you know you've been a sinner and
you're sorry. Then thank Him for letting His Son,
Jesus Christ, take the punishment you deserved—
death. He'll forgive you for everything you've done

wrong and you'll be God's child. That's what being a Christian means. After that, you'll know why lying is wrong and you won't even want to do it any more."

Sharon did not give any answer, but she let Lori know that she didn't want to discuss it further. She took off her housecoat and crawled into bed. "G'night."

"Good night, Sharon."

Lori read a chapter from the Bible and bowed her head to pray, asking God to work in Sharon's life.

The *Betty Jo* traveled steadily all night. Captain Ellis and Rusty took turns at the wheel, navigating the cumbersome houseboat downstream to the place on the chart that Cliff Adams had marked. Shortly before daylight the captain knocked briskly on Cliff's stateroom door.

"Adams!" his resonant voice called out, waking Lori and Sharon as well as Cliff. "Adams, we're here. What do you want us to do now?"

Lori's dad stirred sleepily. "What is it?"

Captain Ellis repeated his question.

"Hold on. I'll be right out."

The two girls lay awake for a few minutes, staring up at the ceiling. At last Lori reached over and switched on the light.

"What are you going to do?" Sharon wanted to know, blinking to keep out the sudden light. "It isn't morning yet."

"It's close to it." Lori swung her feet over the side of the bed. "Besides, everyone else is up."

"Except me." She yawned deeply.

"And you're not going to stay there very long. Come on, Sharon. Let's get up."

"I don't see why," she grumbled. "It's still the middle of the night."

In spite of what she said, Sharon was out of bed, scrambling into her clothes before Lori was dressed. They were both in the wheelhouse when Mr. Adams arrived there.

"I didn't figure you'd all be up so early," Captain Ellis said. "All I wanted to know was what you want me to do now—if you want me to anchor here or go ashore at the landing a mile downstream."

Cliff checked the chart before amswering. "I think maybe it would be a good idea to go half a mile and pull out of the main channel and anchor until we've had breakfast and get ready to go to work."

The captain grunted his approval. "Suits me. Just so I know what you want to do."

Shortly after eight o'clock that morning the *Betty Jo* lifted anchor and began to move upstream.

"How do they plan to find the sunken riverboat without a diver?" Sharon asked.

Lori shrugged. "I don't know for sure. Let's go in where Dad and Captain Ellis are working and see if we can find out."

In the wheelhouse the two men were examining a sophisticated-looking instrument.

"Now, that's the finest depth-sounder I've ever

seen," Captain Ellis said. "You say it records the depth on paper?"

"That's right. Actually, it makes a continuous graph. By keeping the speed of the engines constant and keeping a close check on our location at all times, we can plot our exact position at the time the depth-sounder has recorded any given depth."

"I see you've given some thought to this part of the project."

Cliff grinned. "Actually, I consulted some people in Florida who do a great deal of salvage work. This is one of their methods for locating sunken ships or cargo."

"I guess it doesn't matter whose idea it is, it's a good one."

Cliff set the depth-sounder on a small table in the wheelhouse, ran the transducer cable out the nearest porthole and clamped the transducer to the hull by means of suction cups. Fascinated, Lori and Sharon watched him get the depth-sounder set up. It wasn't long until the pen on the depth-sounder began to squiggle across the narrow graph paper. He made several small adjustments and informed Captain Ellis that they were ready to go to work.

"All right now," the skipper said, "suppose we go over this again from the top, so I'll have it clear in my mind just what you want me to do."

"We're going to work this half-mile stretch first." Cliff indicated an area of the river on the chart.

"We'll move back and forth over this stretch of river, working our way a few feet west on each trip."

The captain nodded. "That's the way I had it doped out, but I wanted to be sure."

Lori and Sharon had imagined the work would be exciting. It was just the opposite. The houseboat inched painstakingly downstream with Cliff marking her progress on the chart. At the prescribed location they came about and chugged back upstream at the same speed. Only the harder pulling of the engines indicated they were fighting against the current.

A few minutes later the turn was repeated and they moved downhill once more.

The girls found the ever moving recorder indicater on the depth-sounder fascinating and slipped into the wheelhouse from time to time to look over Cliff's shoulder.

"Are you finding anything, Dad?"

He shook his head. "There are some variations in depth and certain activity that we really can't account for, but as far as I can tell, we haven't found a thing."

The day dragged by slowly, but at last the time came for them to quit until the next morning.

"I thought sure we'd have found something by this time," Rusty complained.

"It would have been nice," Cliff said, "but we've got to remember that the *Margaret L* has been on the bottom of the river for more than a hundred years and a lot of people have looked for her without finding her. So the chances are against our coming out to this area and locating the old riverboat the first day."

"I suppose you're right, but I thought we'd at least find *something*."

The second and third days were a repetition of the first. They set to work early in the morning, as soon as it was light enough for them to see well, and kept at it until dusk.

The girls spent quite a little time in the wheelhouse at first, watching the depth-sounder chart the bottom of that section of the river, or talking with Mr. Adams as he continually plotted and marked their course. Eventually they tired of that and read or stretched out on the sun deck, soaking up the warmth of the early summer days and trying for a tan.

Strangely, or so it seemed to Lori, Buford Kelly and Tim Nickerson did not put in an appearance. "And I really thought they would be down here almost by the time we arrived," she told her friend.

"So did I. In fact, I thought they would follow us."

"Maybe they weren't really trying to catch us the other day in Omaha," Lori murmured, turning on her side and squinting at Sharon. "Maybe it was just a coincidence that we happened to see them on that corner."

"Oh no, it was more than that." Sharon shuddered. "They were after us! We both couldn't have been mistaken about that."

The *Betty Jo* negotiated another turn. The girls fell silent until the houseboat was creeping north once more.

"You know, Sharon, it could be that they are around here after all."

The other girl sat up quickly. "Now why did you have to say that?"

Lori sat up and, shading her eyes with her sunburned hand, she studied the trees that lined the shore.

"I just realized that anyone who knows what we're doing, like Mr. Kelly and Mr. Nickerson, could tell by watching us that we haven't found anything yet. We wouldn't keep going back and forth if we had."

Sharon scanned the shore too. "You're right, Lori. They could be somewhere on the riverbank watching us."

In spite of the warmth of the afternoon, Lori shivered. Those two men were probably out there right now, studying every move of the houseboat. They wouldn't make a move or even show themselves until her dad found the sunken riverboat. Then they would try to get to it and take it away from them. "They won't get away with it!" she exploded.

Sharon gasped and surprise widened her eyes. "Who's not going to get away with what?" she demanded.

"Kelly and Nickerson are not going to get away with stealing the *Margaret L* from us!"

"What are we going to do about it if they try?"

Lori fell silent. "I don't know," she said at last. "But we can't let them steal the riverboat. We've got to stop them somehow!"

6

A Robbery

Lori and Sharon kept watching the riverbank for some sign that the two men were spying on the *Betty Jo.* But if they were, they were awfully clever about it; not once did they show themselves. Gradually the girls relaxed from their watching. Before the week was out the idea of Kelly and Nickerson swooping down on them like hawks was all but forgotten.

They went ashore once for fuel and supplies, and a second time so Cliff could go to town and phone his diver again to find out when he would be arriving.

"Why does it matter if he's here?" Lori asked. "We don't really need him yet, do we?"

Frowning, Cliff shook his head. "I guess we don't need him here, at that. But I want to be sure that he's around when we do need him. When we find the *Margaret L,* I don't want any further delays." He checked his address book to be sure that he had Frank McMillan's number. "I'll be back in a couple of hours, Lori."

"Do you want us to go with you?"

"No, not this time," he said quickly. "You'd better stay on board." There was a warning tone in his voice.

"Why?" The word popped out before she could stop it.

"I just think it's best, that's all." His tone also implied, "And don't ask any more questions."

She promised to do as he asked.

Sharon, who was standing nearby, watched him leave the dock and stride in the direction of the little town of Grenville, Nebraska.

"Your dad thinks Kelly and Nickerson are around here too," she said at last. "He's afraid they're watching every move we make."

Lori flinched. Sharon might very well be right. Her dad must have had some reason for insisting that they stay on board the houseboat.

She still had not spoken when Rusty came swaggering up to them. "Well, I see you're still around."

"And where did you expect us to be?" Sharon demanded.

"To tell you the truth, I thought maybe you had curled up and died of boredom."

"We manage to get by," Lori replied.

He laughed. "As far as I'm concerned, this trip has been a big fat bore from the start."

"I'm sorry you find it so dull. The next time we charter your houseboat we'll try to provide a little more entertainment for you."

"That would help." He leaned against the railing, surveying first one and then the other. "Do you have any ideas for right now?"

"This is your boat and your river," Sharon reminded him coldly. "Do *you* have any ideas about what we could do for a little entertainment?"

He took his time answering. "There are some big catfish in the river," he told her. "We could go fishing."

"That would be something to do," Lori said. "What do you think, Sharon?"

"About fishing?" She wrinkled her nose distastefully. "Ugh!"

"If you don't want to fish, how about swimming?"

"In this dirty water? No, thank you."

Lori saw for the first time that in spite of all his teasing, Rusty was actually serious about finding something that they would enjoy doing.

"Thank you anyway," Lori said.

"Thanks? I haven't done anything yet."

"I appreciate your wanting to."

"We wouldn't want anyone to die of boredom on the *Betty Jo*. That would be bad for business."

"Keep trying. Maybe you'll come up with something."

"All afternoon I've been trying to think of things that you might like to do. But you don't want to go fishing or swimming. The only other thing I can think of is to go back to that old abandoned tug that's pulled up on shore a couple of miles upriver. We could explore that."

Interest made the girls' eyes sparkle. "Are you sure it would be all right?" Lori asked cautiously.

"I don't know why not. It's been there for more years than I can remember. Of course, it might not be an old tug at all. Maybe it's the *Margaret L* in disguise." He wiggled his eyebrows and tried to look mysterious.

They both laughed.

"How about that? Wouldn't it be something if the old riverboat was in plain view on shore all along and nobody recognized it?"

Sharon scowled, but Lori laughed at his attempts at humor.

"I'm glad I thought about that old tugboat. We've got to go back and explore it. Who knows? It may make me a hero." His smile disappeared. "I really am serious. We could take the dinghy and go back and explore that old tugboat. Every time we've gone by it I've wanted to stop and take a look inside."

"We can't go now," Lori said. "We told Dad we wouldn't leave the *Betty Jo* while he's gone tonight."

"It's too late to go tonight anyway," he said. "It'll take quite a while to go up there and look the boat over and come back."

With that he left them abruptly and went back to the wheelhouse.

"What do you suppose was the matter with him?" Sharon asked. "It isn't like him to be so nice all of a sudden."

"We ought to be glad he's agreeable."

"I would be if I trusted him, but I don't. He's got some reason for trying to be so nice to us." Sharon paused thoughtfully. "I'd like to know what it is."

The girls expected Cliff to be back shortly after dark although he did not tell them when to expect him when he left. Ten o'clock came and went and he still had not returned.

"You don't suppose he was stopped by those two hoods, do you?" Lori asked with concern.

"More likely, he's had trouble calling Mr. McMillan. He could be waiting at the phone to get his call through."

"I suppose you're right, but I can't help feeling a little uneasy."

They waited up until ten-thirty before deciding to go to bed. "I don't think I'll be able to sleep until Dad gets back aboard," Lori said.

Nevertheless, she did lie down and finally dozed in a light sleep. The next thing she knew, a muffled sound was drifting in to them from the stateroom next to them. It was so faint that she could not be sure that she had heard anything at all.

She opened her eyes sleepily and listened, lying still in her bed.

A moment later she heard it again, the footsteps of someone in her dad's stateroom and the sound of drawers being pulled out.

She raised herself on one elbow, straining to separate the stealthy sounds from the hush of the night. Whoever was in the stateroom didn't want to alarm anyone else on the houseboat. Lori thought Sharon was still asleep until her friend spoke.

"Lori! Lori!" Her voice was tense.

"What is it?"

"Do—do you hear somebody in your dad's room?" The silence was deafening. "Whoever it is just woke me up."

The girls both listened and the sounds came again.

"Maybe your dad came back and is getting ready for bed," Sharon suggested hopefully.

Lori wanted to believe that, too. She was as anxious as Sharon to find some simple, logical explanation for being awakened. But, she realized with sudden concern, whoever was in that stateroom didn't belong there. He was pulling out too many drawers and opening too many doors. It sounded to her as though someone must have sneaked aboard the *Betty Jo* and was going through everything in it.

"That isn't Dad in there," she whispered.

"Are you sure?"

"I'm positive. He wouldn't be making as much noise as that." By this time she had swung her feet over the side of the bed and stood erect. "It sounds to me like Dad's visitor is looking for something Dad has, or he *thinks* Dad has."

"W-w-what are you going to do?" the other girl whispered.

Lori slipped into her robe. How could she answer Sharon? She didn't really know what to do. Her mind seemed to churn until she could scarcely think. At the moment all she realized was that somebody was going through her dad's stateroom, somebody who didn't belong there!

"I'm going to go and get Captain Ellis," she whispered.

"Captain Ellis!" Sharon's voice raised.

"Shh!" But it was too late. The person in the room next to theirs froze for an instant. Then they heard the door being flung open and the sound of feet running the length of the houseboat. There was a splash as though whoever had been aboard jumped into the water. Then all was silent.

"He's gone!" Lori cried in dismay. "He's gone!"

Sharon was breathing heavily. She was the one who had frightened the intruder away. "I—I'm sorry. I was so excited I wasn't thinking straight. I guess I didn't even think he could hear me."

Lori felt her own temper surge as she thought about what Sharon had done. But, she soon realized, being angry with her friend wasn't going to change anything. The harm had already been done and nothing could undo it.

"It's just as well," she said, shrugging. "I don't know what would have happened if we had surprised that man in Dad's room." She shuddered. "It could have been a lot worse than it is now. I'm sure of that."

By this time Captain Ellis and Rusty, awakened by the commotion, came hurrying down to the girls' room, pounding on the door.

"What's going on in there?" the captain demanded. "Are you all right?"

"I think so." Lori opened the door.

"What was it? Who was making all the noise?"

"We don't know. Somebody was in Dad's room. We heard him."

Captain Ellis pursed his lips. "To tell you the truth, I'm not surprised. After that article in the paper I was sure that somebody would be trying something like this. The amount of gold bullion that's rumored to be on the *Margaret L* is enough to arouse the greed in a lot of men."

"Do you suppose they got anything from Mr. Adams' room?" Rusty asked.

"Maybe we'd better go in and take a look."

The lights revealed that Cliff Adams' stateroom had, indeed, been ransacked. All the dresser drawers had been jerked out and emptied onto the bed. The desk drawer had been removed and even the wastebasket had been overturned in a frantically thorough search.

"Whoever was in here was pretty anxious to find what he was looking for," Captain Ellis said, letting his anger show in his face.

"But, did the thief find what he was looking for?" Sharon wanted to know.

The skipper of the houseboat glanced at her.

"The only person who can give us the answer to that is Cliff Adams. None of the rest of us even know what was in here, let alone what's still here."

They were still in Mr. Adams' stateroom when Cliff came back aboard the *Betty Jo.* He looked about quickly. "What's this all about? What happened?"

"Suppose you tell us." The captain took a deep breath. "It looks to me like somebody is mighty anxious to get his hands on something that you've got. Or maybe he's got it now."

Even before Captain Ellis quit talking, Cliff was on his way to the closet. He flung open the door, dropped to his knees, and began to rummage through the luggage inside.

"It's gone!" he cried.

Four pairs of eyes were staring at him as he hunched there for a moment before straightening and turning to look at them.

"It's gone!" he half whispered.

"What is it, Dad? What were they after?"

He came back numbly to where the others were

standing. "They stole my copy of the original log of the *Margaret L* that the Nebraska Historical Society made for me."

"Oh well," Captain Ellis said, "if you only had a copy, there's nothing to worry about. They didn't get too much."

"It's not quite as simple as that." Cliff dropped heavily to a chair. "You see, the historical society didn't realize they had the log stuck away in their archives until I began to press them for it. I knew it existed because I found reference to it during my research. I asked them to keep it under wraps because of all the wild talk about the gold bullion the riverboat was supposed to have had in the cargo, and the fact that the log pinpointed the area where the *Margaret L* went down more accurately than any other material that had been discovered up to this point."

"I see."

"So, they had a copy of the log made for me to use as a guide to start my search, and they were going to keep the log away from the general public."

"Seems as though they were giving you the advantage, doesn't it?" Ellis asked.

"I guess it does when you look at it that way, but they had their reasons for it. You see, I discovered the existence of the log and kept after them until they located it. That was the first thing. More important, the others who were looking for the *Margaret L* were doing so for personal profit. The aims of the historical society and our expedition were the same. We both wanted to find the sunken riverboat, restore the artifacts that are aboard her, and see that they are preserved for their historical value. And if the Carstigan diary is found, that alone would be worth the whole trip."

Cliff pulled in a deep breath. "But now it's gone! I've lost any advantage I would have had in finding the sunken riverboat before anyone else does."

Lori and Sharon's concern was stamped on their faces.

Captain Ellis turned abruptly. "Come on, Rusty. Let's get to bed. There's nothing else we can do until morning."

For a brief time Cliff stared at the closet as though still trying to comprehend what had actually taken place in his stateroom.

"What are we going to do now, Dad?" Lori asked, her voice hushed. "Are we going to have to give up searching for the *Margaret L*?"

He stood slowly to his feet. "No, we're not going to give up. That would be the same as turning the riverboat over to Kelly and Nickerson and I'm not about to do that."

They waited for him to continue but he didn't.

"What are we going to do?" she repeated.

"I don't know." His voice was distant and he sounded discouraged.

7

A Dangerous Encounter

The following morning Cliff and Captain Ellis discussed the advisability of notifying the sheriff of the theft aboard the *Betty Jo*.

"I don't think we've got any choice. We're supposed to tell the authorities when there's been an infraction of the law," Mr. Adams pointed out.

"That's just the way I feel. I'll take care of it this morning," the captain agreed.

"Good. Would you take me back to the marina? I'll have to pick up the car and drive to Lincoln for another copy of the log."

"Sure, Cliff."

Lori thought about that. It was good that her dad would be able to replace the material that was so important to him, but it did mean that they would lose a day or two.

"In a way, it gives Kelly and Nickerson or whoever stole that log from you the advantage of a day, doesn't it?"

Cliff nodded slowly. "It gives them a start of at least a day. But there's nothing we can do about that now. They've got it and the chances are we're not going to be able to get it away from them."

Cliff arose to leave. "I've got to go through the county seat on the way to Lincoln. I'll stop and see the sheriff personally and have him come out."

Cliff left the *Betty Jo,* striding purposefully off the dock and along the road in the direction of the town.

"I wish he didn't have to go," Lori said wistfully.

"So do I. It's sort of scary here without him."

The girls didn't think Rusty had heard them until he spoke. "That's no way to talk. *I'm* here to take care of you."

"I'm sorry," Lori teased. "I'd forgotten all about you."

"Now I am crushed. I think I'll go to my room and cry. And to think, I was going to tell you that I'm ready to take you upriver to visit the old tug." They could tell his "disappointment" was only put on.

They were still on deck talking, when a large open boat came roaring downstream to a spot almost even with them and cut speed.

"What do you think they're going to do?" Sharon asked in a tense whisper.

"They're probably just fishermen," Rusty replied.

But Lori wasn't so sure. "They're right out there where we've been working."

Rusty drew in a deep breath. "You know, you've got a point there. Of course, they could be trolling."

"And they could be using that log that was stolen from Dad to try and locate the sunken riverboat," Lori said. "I wish he was back."

Captain Ellis had been watching the boat too. He

came to the door and called to Rusty and the girls. "Come here a minute, will you?"

He motioned them into the wheelhouse.

"I see that you noticed our friends out there," he said, subconsciously keeping his voice low.

"At first I thought they were fishing," Rusty said. "Then I realized that the girls are right. They're doing exactly like we've been doing and in the same place."

The captain nodded in agreement. "There's no doubt in my mind that they've got Cliff's copy of the log."

Lori glanced out the window at the slowly moving boat, trying to see whether Kelly and Nickerson were the ones who had just moved into their area.

"What are we going to do about it?" she asked. "Will we go out and see if they have it?"

The captain frowned. "We wouldn't have any right to do that. And besides, that would alert them to the fact that we suspect them." He picked up his cap and jammed it on his head. "I think I'll have to go below anyway, and phone the sheriff so he hurries out here while those characters are still here. Be careful, and don't stand around on the deck watching them. Just do whatever you would normally do if they were a thousand miles away."

In a few minutes the captain returned. "Sheriff says we don't have enough evidence to call him out here. They haven't bothered us yet, so until they do, there's no way he can help us." He shook his head.

"Well, I guess I'd better get that chart work done that I had to put off before. It can't wait forever. You kids keep an eye on that boat. I'll be down below the rest of the afternoon."

They watched the boat for a while. Then Sharon broke the silence. "I wonder if that is Kelly and Nickerson out in that boat."

"I couldn't answer that right now," Rusty said, looking from one to the other significantly. "But if you talk real nice to me, I just might be kindhearted enough to gas up the motor on the dinghy and take you out by that boat on our way upriver to the tug."

Excitement widened Lori's eyes. "*Would* you?"

"You aren't serious about that, are you?" Sharon broke in incredulously. "You *really* wouldn't be stupid enough to go close to those men so we could see who's out there, would you?"

"I just might if everybody is extra nice to me."

Lori was thinking about something else. She took a short breath and exhaled it with a rush. "It might help if we got some pictures of them. That might be the evidence the sheriff says he needs."

"Pictures now, she says!" Sharon grasped her forehead in mock agony. "The next thing I suppose, you'll want to go aboard and talk to them."

"I hadn't thought of that," her friend answered, "but it is something to consider."

Sharon shook her head. "I don't know why I didn't let well enough alone and stay at home when I was there."

"You're as anxious as I am to find out who's out in that boat."

"Oh no I'm not. I'd rather stay here and guess."

"We're not going to be able to find out a thing unless we get a move on." Rusty strode to the door. "I'll gas up the outboard and we'll be ready to go in ten minutes, OK?" With that he left them alone.

Sharon waited until the door closed behind him before turning to face her friend.

"This is crazy, Lori. There's no knowing what those two men might do."

"We aren't going to get *that* close to them."

"All right," Sharon exclaimed when she saw that Lori was not to be dissuaded. "All right. We'll go out there! But when we get into trouble, don't say that I didn't warn you."

They went to the stern of the houseboat just as Rusty finished filling the outboard tank with gas.

"Are you ready?" Lori asked, whispering although the boat was half a mile away.

"As ready as I'll ever be."

She glanced across the water at the open fishing boat apprehensively. Going out to have a close look at the men in the other boat had seemed like such a good idea a few moments ago. Now, however, she wasn't so sure.

What if it was Kelly and Nickerson? What would they do then?

The two girls got into the aluminum boat with

Rusty, who started the outboard and moved slowly away from the *Betty Jo.*

Lori fumbled nervously with her camera. She wished she had a telephoto lens so they wouldn't have to get so near for the picture. She wondered what the men out there would do when they saw her camera.

Rusty seemed as reluctant to approach the fishing boat as the girls. He fumbled with the carburator adjustment and ran at half-throttle.

Lori's pulse quickened as the dinghy drew closer to the open boat. There were two men in the other craft. One was at the steering wheel and the other was bent over something in the midsection. At first the men did not seem to notice that the smaller boat was closing in on them.

The kids couldn't tell whether the men were Kelly and Nickerson or not. The one at the steering wheel had a cap jammed over his eyes and the other kept his head down.

"Get that camera ready," Rusty ordered. "I may have to peel out of here in a big hurry."

They were still at least three hundred yards away when the men realized they were coming toward them. For an instant the two men remained motionless. Then they stood straight up and stared at the *Betty Jo.*

Kelly and Nickerson! There was no mistaking them.

Lori raised her camera.

At that instant Kelly, who was the steering wheel, sat down and opened the throttle. The big open boat lurched forward with a suddenness that almost threw Nickerson off his feet. It skidded as it came about, gathering speed as it aimed directly for them.

"Look out!" Sharon cried. "They're going to run us down!"

The boat roared toward them on a collision course. The girls both screamed and covered their eyes with their hands.

Rusty shoved hard on the motor handle, opening the throttle as he did so. The dinghy canted dangerously as it swerved ninety degrees, allowing the fishing boat to barely knife past. The wake of the heavy boat sent water spilling over the gunwale, dumping two inches in the bottom. With that Kelly and Nickerson roared away.

The girls and their companion stared after the other boat, half fearful that it would turn and come charging back at them once more.

"Whew!" Rusty exclaimed. "That was a close one."

Lori was still trembling. "I thought we were goners for sure."

"What are we going to do now?" Sharon asked at last.

Rusty glanced over his shoulder, as though to make sure that Kelly and his friend Nickerson kept on going.

"Well, we could go on upriver and explore that old tugboat," he said, "in case you haven't had enough excitement for one day."

"I don't know." Sharon shook her head nervously. "I'm not sure that I feel like taking that trip."

"I know what's eating you," he said, a smile playing at the corners of his mouth. "You're all shook up, aren't you?"

"Who wouldn't be?"

"Me, for example. Those guys wouldn't have run you down. They just wanted to scare you good." He laughed. "And it looks to me like they really did."

Sharon bristled and drew in a breath between her teeth. *"We're* not afraid to do anything that *you're* not afraid to do, buddy."

"That's great. Then there's not a thing to keep us from going up to the old abandoned boat."

The girls eyed each other. It wasn't quite what they wanted to do, but they didn't have any choice unless they wanted to have Rusty razzing them about getting scared. By the time they resigned themselves to the fact that they were going up to the tug whether they wanted to or not, they were a mile from the open boat.

Kelly and Nickerson were acting as though there was no one else within a hundred miles of their fishing boat. They were in practically the same location where they had been before, moving carefully downstream.

"I just happened to think of something," Lori said.

"We left the *Betty Jo*; Captain Ellis is still down below deck. You don't suppose that Kelly and Nickerson will go aboard while we're gone, do you?"

"They might, at that," Sharon said quickly. "Maybe we ought to turn around and go back."

Rusty's laughter rang. "You really are scared, aren't you?"

"What do you mean by that?" she demanded.

"You'd do almost anything to keep from going aboard that old boat, wouldn't you, Sharon?"

She jerked herself erect indignantly. "You really think you know everything." She paused for a moment. "For your information I was only thinking about your old houseboat. If you don't care whether it's broken into again then I don't either. I was only trying to protect your property."

"Come off it now," he said, waving his right hand. "You know that I was only kidding."

"Didn't sound like that to me."

"Well, you're wrong."

Sharon pouted until they drew alongside the old tug.

"Have you ever been aboard her?" Lori asked.

Rusty shook his head. "The closest I've been is the river channel. But I've always wanted to stop and explore it."

"I like to do that sort of thing too," Lori told him.

Rusty cut off the motor and they glided in the direction of the old tug.

"Catch us!" Rusty cried, "so we don't hit too hard!"

Sharon turned and put out her hands to fend the little dinghy away from the broad bow of the tug. As they were about to thud into the tug boat an old, cracking voice rasped out. "Avast there! Avast! This here's private property!"

The girls both shuddered. Even Rusty caught his breath sharply. "I—I didn't know there was anyone here!"

"So you thought you'd come aboard and strip my boat bare, eh?"

All three of them were staring at the aging hull, questions spinning through their minds.

"W-who is he, Rusty?" Lori whispered.

"I don't have the slightest idea. I've never seen anyone here before."

"How do we know this boat belongs to you?" she demanded.

Lori's question stopped him.

"This boat's *mine*," he repeated firmly. "So, just be on your way before I lose my temper."

"Let's go," Rusty said under his breath.

Lori shook her head. "As far as we know, we've got just as much right here as you have."

There was a long silence.

"You've got spunk, young'un. I'll say that for you. You've got plenty of spunk!" His laugh sounded more like a cackle.

8

Amazing Discoveries

Lori and Sharon eyed each other questioningly. What sort of a man was this who would live on an abandoned tugboat on the banks of the Missouri River? His quavering, gravelly voice did not sound ominous in spite of the harshness of his words. But what was he doing here by himself? And why would he question them as though he owned the boat?

They still had not moved when a gaunt, shadowy figure hobbled into view and a whiskery face peered down at them. "Suppose you young'uns just come aboard now and let me take a good look-see at you."

"I don't think we ought to," Sharon whispered. "Do you?"

The stranger moved another step forward and lowered himself to his knees. Bony, arthritic fingers reached over the stern of the battered tug. "Hand me your line, young lady, and I'll make it fast so's your boat won't drift away."

Lori, who was the nearest to the anchor rope, drew back instinctively and glanced at Rusty once more. He looked helpless. Before he could react, the old man was speaking again.

"Don't you get me riled up, young women. I'm a terror when I'm riled."

"I—I—" She bent and reached uncertainly for the rope.

"Hand that line up here and be quick about it!"

Lori did as she was told.

"There now!" The old man cackled. "Let me give you a hand and help you aboard. It's been a powerful long time since the *Wren* and me had ourselves any company."

Because they could think of nothing else to do they followed his instructions. Lori was the first to clamber out of the dinghy, placing her firm young hand into the old man's twisted fingers.

"Up we go!"

She was astonished at the strength in the elderly man's arm. He raised her easily, as though she had been half her weight. She could imagine the power of that muscular frame when he was only twice her age. While he helped Sharon climb out of the dinghy to the deck of the tug, Lori moved to the center, surveying the ancient boat with curiosity.

There was no doubt of it. The old man lived aboard the tug. The windows in the little cabin were clean, and somebody had hung curtains at them a long time ago.

"Now you, young fella! Get up here and be quick about it!"

When Rusty was aboard the *Wren* the stranger thrust out his hand. "I'm Amos Jefferson. *Captain*

Amos Jefferson, the skipper of the best and fastest tugboat ever to twist a screw in the muddy waters of the old Missouri."

Rusty introduced himself and the girls.

"I'm right honored to have you aboard," Amos said, a grin briefly showing his scraggly teeth. "There ain't been a female set foot on the *Wren* since Winnie died nineteen years ago." His voice broke. "As a matter of fact there ain't been hardly anybody come to see old Amos the last few years."

Lori felt sorry for him. And to think that she had been afraid of the lonely old man.

"There's no use in our standing out here," he said. "Let's go in where you can be comfortable whilst I whump up some tea."

They followed him into the galley of the tug and sat down. "Yes sirree, when I got up this morning I knowed this was goin' to be a good day. I knowed it in my bones." He hobbled over to the stove and lit a burner. "I says to myself, 'Amos Jefferson, you'd just as well h'ist your weary bones outa that bunk. You're goin' to have a good day for a change'." His watery eyes gleamed. "And look what's happened already. Comp'ny's come."

Over a cup of tea they talked about the things Amos had seen along the river in the early days.

"There ain't nothin' I don't know about this here river," he said. "I know when she's happy and when she's sad." His eyes showed his mood change to sadness. "I've seen good men drown right whilst I was watchin' 'em. Men who knowed this here river as good as I do. She snatched our only son from our arms. That's what she did. An' we never so much as found the body afterwards."

"How terrible!" Lori reacted without thinking.

"Yes, sir. It hit Winnie right hard, that did. I don't rightly think she ever got over it. It sort of killed somethin' down inside of her. She wasn't the same after that."

"When was that?"

His sunken eyes clouded and for a moment he was transported back in time. "Let's see now, it's been a long, long time ago," he began. "I don't rightly know, but it was before the big flood. I can remember coming into the shipping channel below Miller's Point and asking Will to keep a weather eye for barges. A skipper with barges in tow don't pay no 'tention to nobody. They'd better get out of his way iffen they don't want to tangle with him.

"Then that storm hit and I was plumb busy for a couple of hours. Didn't even know the little boy had been washed overboard until the storm was over an' we was almost back at the dock."

"In Omaha?" Rusty asked.

"I should say not. At this next town just below us—Grenville." His voice faltered.

Grenville was where the *Betty Jo* was secured.

"What happened next?" Sharon broke in.

"Nothing, really. I docked at the foot of Main Street and went into town to report it to the sheriff.

When I got back Winnie was in bed. Wouldn't eat nothin' or say a word. Just laid there without moving any more than she had to. And when she finally got up she wasn't the same person that she had been before. The life had gone out of her." He poured them more tea. "She lived for quite a while after that, but I don't think I ever saw her smile again."

"That must have been awful for both of you." Sharon's voice was hushed.

Something that Amos said about docking the boat didn't ring true to Lori, but she thought it would be rude to question the old man. He'd probably just gotten his facts mixed up. So she let it go.

"But I've bored you enough with my troubles. When you've finished your tea I'll show you around." He paused, surveying the boat he called home. "I've got the *Wren* fixed up pretty good for an old tub. Of course, she's retired, just like me. Neither one of us are much good for anything any more."

He took them through the battered tugboat, showing them the wheelhouse and the rusted engine below. The old tug still had a square, sturdy look but close inspection of the hull showed the evidences of age and wear.

"She must have been quite a boat," Rusty said admiringly, running a hand along the rusted railing.

"She was that." The old man beamed. "There wasn't another tug on the river that could do more work than she could. Anyone'll tell you that."

Before they left, Amos Jefferson invited them back.

"You just come any time. It gets mighty lonesome around here."

As Rusty and the girls neared the place where the big houseboat was docked, they could see that Kelly and Nickerson had anchored on the near side of the shipping channel and had a diver in the water.

"Look over there!" Lori cried, with dismay. "They've got a man diving! They must have located the *Margaret L* already!"

"Or," Sharon added, "maybe they just *think* they have found the old riverboat."

Her friend did little to ease the concern that was weighing on Lori.

Rusty's grin widened. "How about it? Do either of you want to go out and get some pictures of their diver in action?"

"No, thank you!" the girls answered in unison.

They cut their speed and angled up to the *Betty Jo.* Lori was staring across the murky water at the anchored fishing boat.

"Dad said he'd send the sheriff out to arrest them for breaking into his stateroom," she muttered under her breath. "I wonder what happened to him."

"Maybe he hasn't gotten here yet."

"He should have been here long before this," Lori continued.

Captain Ellis came out and held the dinghy while

the girls clambered on deck. "I'm glad you're back. I was beginning to get concerned about you."

Rusty told him where they had been.

"What about the sheriff?" Lori asked. "Wasn't he going to arrest those men?"

"He came out," the captain said, "and went over the stateroom, but he couldn't make any arrests. He didn't have any evidence that would involve those two."

Lori found it difficult to believe him. "But they must have Dad's copy of the log out in their boat right now. That ought to be proof enough."

"He couldn't even search their boat without a warrant," Captain Ellis went on. "As a matter of fact, if they saw him coming they could scoot over to the other side of the river and they would be in Iowa and out of the Nebraska sheriff's jurisdiction." He paused for a moment. "No, he is going to have to have a lot more evidence than he's got right now or he won't be able to do a thing about arresting them."

Lori groaned aloud. This was worse than she had supposed it could be. Those two men could go right on looking for the *Margaret L*, using the log her dad discovered, and there wasn't a thing that he would be able to do about it.

An hour later the fishing boat still had not moved, except to swing from side to side with the current. Lori and Sharon were in their stateroom watching from behind the drapes when a station wagon drove up and two men got out.

"Dad!" Lori cried, running to meet him. "Dad!"

Cliff eyed the boat in the middle of the river with uneasiness. "Who's that?"

"Who would you guess it to be?" the captain asked.

Concern removed his smile. "How long have they been here?"

"Since shortly after you left. And the sheriff said he couldn't do a thing about it. He couldn't find a bit of evidence that would tie Kelly and Nickerson to the theft of the log from your stateroom."

He frowned. "I should have known." Then his face brightened again. "There's no use in getting so shook up about that. We're ready to go to work now, ourselves." He turned to his companion. "This is Frank McMillan."

Lori and the others shook hands with the diver enthusiastically.

"Yes," Cliff went on, stepping aboard the houseboat. "Things worked out very well. I picked up another copy of the log in Lincoln and, when I tried to call Frank, I couldn't get him. His wife said he was on his way to Omaha. So I drove over there and met his flight and here we are."

He tried to act as though the worst of the problem was over, but they all knew that it wasn't. It was only beginning. They not only had to find the sunken riverboat, but they had to do it before Kelly and Nickerson did. And that wasn't going to be easy.

It wasn't long until the other diver scrambled out

of the water into the open boat. Nickerson lifted the anchor and they went roaring noisily upstream. Lori and Sharon watched them go with growing satisfaction.

"At least they must not have found anything valuable on the bottom today," Sharon said. "If they had, they wouldn't have quit so early."

"Maybe," Lori replied. She hoped that Sharon was right and that the men in the other boat hadn't found what they were looking for. But the fact that they broke off the search early didn't prove anything. It could be that they had located the *Margaret L* and were on their way back to Omaha to get a barge with a boom to help in the salvage operation.

"What do you think we'll do now?"

Lori shook her head. "I haven't the faintest idea."

The next morning Cliff woke everyone up as the sun poked its glimmering face above the horizon.

"Why do you want us up so early?" Sharon grumbled, rubbing the sleep from her eyes with her fists.

"I want you to go in and help Rusty get breakfast right away. We've got a lot of work to do today. Let's get with it."

Even before the breakfast dishes were finished, Captain Ellis took the *Betty Jo* out into the river and they set to work. The morning was a repeat of the other days when they had been looking for the sunken riverboat. They made their way back and forth over the area, watching the moving needle on the depth-sounder.

It wasn't long until the open boat came back, knifing through the water at top speed.

"Oh-oh," Cliff murmured under his breath. "It looks like we've got company."

The man in the other boat did not glance toward the *Betty Jo*, but they slid to a stop not far away and dropped anchor. A moment later their diver went over the side.

"You know something," Rusty said under his breath, "those guys act like they know exactly what they're doing."

Lori did not answer him, but she had to admit that they gave every indication of knowing where to look for the *Margaret L*.

"Do you suppose they really have found the riverboat?" Sharon asked.

Rusty tugged at his ear lobe. "I wouldn't know, but they sure act like they've located something." His teasing smile came back. "And, Lori, for your benefit I can tell you that they *don't* think it's historical artifacts."

Sharon nodded her agreement. Lori could say all she wanted to about the sort of items her dad was interested in getting off the *Margaret L*, and that he would tell them if he was actually after the gold bullion. Lori could believe if she wanted to that her dad was a Christian and wouldn't lie because of it. But Lori didn't need to try to get her to believe it too. Sharon knew better. Cliff Adams was just like everyone else. He was after the million dollars in gold and he didn't care what he did or what he had to say to beat out the others and get it for himself. It didn't make any difference whether he was a Christian or not.

Lori glanced at Rusty and then away quickly. Neither he nor Sharon believed her, she knew that. And there was nothing she could say that would make them believe she was telling the truth.

The open boat lifted anchor after an hour and moved a hundred yards to where they again sent down their diver. After several dives they moved again.

Frank McMillan watched them placidly. "You don't have anything to worry about, Cliff," he said. "Those guys haven't got a thing yet."

"I wish I could be as sure as you are."

"You can be. They haven't put out a marker buoy, for one thing. That's the first and best signal that a diver thinks he's in fertile ground."

"They could be omitting that in order to throw us off."

Mr. McMillan shook his head. "Not a chance. They wouldn't dare risk losing it, if they were really on to something."

The other boat had quit for the day when the *Betty Jo* located something. Cliff stared incredulously at the violently squiggling depth-sounder.

"Stop!" he cried. "Stop!"

Captain Ellis reversed the engines and the houseboat stopped dead in the water.

9

Frustrated Hopes

Lori and Sharon, who had been sunning on deck most of the afternoon, burst breathlessly into the wheelhouse as the cumbersome houseboat lurched to a halt.

"What is it, Dad?"

His eyes showed the excitement that he tried to conceal. "I don't know for sure." He tried to be cautious but with little success. "It's probably too early to tell if it's anything at all, but we do have something most unusual on the depth-sounder."

He showed them the continuous graph that had been coming out of the depth-sounder.

"What is it?" Lori asked, in a low but excited tone. "What happened?"

Before her dad could reply, Captain Ellis broke in. "If you want to stay where we are right now you'd better throw a buoy out or drop anchor. If we don't, the current'll take us away."

"I'll have Rusty get a marker into the water."

Once that was accomplished they dropped anchor.

"Think we've got time to dive before dark?" Cliff asked the diver. Mr. McMillan shook his head. "Not a chance in this murky water. I probably couldn't see a foot in front of my nose. You've got to have bright sunlight in situations like this."

Cliff was not too pleased by his diver's decision not to go down until the next day. But he knew Frank McMillan. There was no use in trying to get the diver to change his mind. He knew the conditions he could dive under safely and refused to go down in anything less.

Cliff was actually glad for that. Diving, especially in a river like the Missouri, was dangerous business. He didn't want to be responsible for sending a man down or having him stay topside.

"I'll go down in the morning and have a look around," Mr. McMillan promised.

"Fine."

Captain Ellis and Cliff both checked to be sure that the plastic bottle Rusty tossed out as a marker was well weighted down, and would stay in place throughout the night. Only then did they move toward the dock, groping their way in the rapidly descending darkness.

"We're going to have to get out here plenty early in the morning," Cliff said to no one in particular. "We've got the marker in place. If those other guys beat us to it, we might be in the position of having found the sunken ship for them."

Lori's eyes were dancing with excitement. "Do

you really think that we've found the *Margaret L?*"
she asked.

"We've found something, that's for sure."

That night Lori and Sharon were so excited they
could scarcely sleep. They lay in bed for an hour or
more, talking in low tones.

"I've been so afraid those men were going to beat
us to it," Lori said.

"So have I," Sharon replied.

"I'd like to see the looks on their faces when *we*
raise the riverboat."

They both laughed. That would shock Kelly and
Nickerson. Those two thought they were so smart!
And they had stolen her dad's copy of the log, Lori
was sure, in spite of the fact that the sheriff couldn't
find enough evidence to accuse them.

If they did find the sunken riverboat and raise her,
it wouldn't make any difference whether Kelly and
his ugly-tempered friend Nickerson were arrested or
not. All her dad really wanted to do was to keep
them from getting to the *Margaret L* before he did.

The next morning the sun was still behind the
distant horizon when Cliff woke everyone up.
"We've got to get back to our marker before anyone
else finds it and starts diving beside it."

As the *Betty Jo* swung about and headed back to
the middle of the turbulent stream, the girls could
hear the deep-throated throb of a big outboard
motor.

"They're coming back!" Lori whispered tensely.

Rusty listened, nodding his agreement. "I think you're right!"

"What can we do about it?" Sharon asked.

"Try to beat them out there and get a diver in the water before they do," he murmured.

The first gray shoots of dawn were streaking the eastern sky as the searchlight on the houseboat probed the swirling river for the marker. Captain Ellis thought he could go directly to the plastic bottle they had tossed out to mark the spot where the depth-sounder wrote a question mark on the graph. But he was wrong. He made three or four passes at it before Rusty spied it twenty-five yards to their starboard.

The open boat was continuing to draw closer. The whine of the racing outboard sounded above the low throbbing of the houseboat's engines. An instant before the other craft burst into view, Captain Ellis shut off the engines and dropped anchor.

"Get that marker out of the water!" Mr. Adams cried. "If those characters spy it they'll know we've found something and give us more trouble than they've been giving us already."

Rusty grabbed up a boathook and raked the bottle over to the houseboat so he could lift it in.

Cliff checked their position on the chart as a final precaution, trying to determine whether the marker had moved downstream during the night, and Mr. McMillan got ready to go down. Kelly brought his boat within a dozen yards of the *Betty Jo* and boldly watched the preparations.

"Just act as though they're nowhere around," Cliff whispered.

Lori felt the color drain from her cheeks and sweat moisten the palms of her hands. It wasn't going to be easy to follow her dad's orders. Not when Kelly and Nickerson were sitting out there like vultures waiting for an opportunity to swoop in and take what they wanted. But with effort, she forced her attention to the diver and her dad.

It was only a moment or two until McMillan adjusted the oxygen tank on his back, checked his mouthpiece, and climbed over the railing. "I'm ready, Cliff," he said crisply.

"Good. Let's get at it."

The diver dropped over the side of the houseboat effortlessly and disappeared from view. Lori and Sharon peered into the swirling, muddy water, tracing the diver's location by the bubbles that came to the surface.

"How long do you think he'll stay down?" Sharon asked uneasily.

"About thirty minutes, I suppose."

The diver in the other boat was getting ready to go below. He tightened the straps on his tanks and slipped his feet into the flippers, working hurriedly.

"I don't know whether I like this or not," Cliff muttered under his breath.

"Isn't there any way that we can stop them from diving when Mr. McMillan is down?" Lori asked.

He shook his head. "Not that I know of. Actually, their man has just as much right to dive as Frank does."

A few minutes later Mr. McMillan came to the surface near the houseboat.

"Find anything?" Lori cried.

Her dad warned her to silence with a stern look. The diver must have heard her, but he made no attempt to speak until he swam over to the *Betty Jo* and was helped aboard. "Man, that's the muddiest water I ever dived in. I couldn't see more than a yard in any direction."

"What about our friend next door?" Cliff asked. "Did you see anything of him?"

Frank shook his head. "I couldn't have seen him unless he'd been sitting on my lap."

The others stood silently around the diver while he lay back, breathing heavily. At last he sat up again.

"Find anything?" Cliff asked.

"There's something down there, all right, but the water's so murky I couldn't tell what it was."

Cliff allowed himself to sound excited. "Think you can lift it with a line?"

"Maybe," Frank McMillan said curtly, "and maybe not. It depends on whether I can get a line under it or not. As soon as I've rested a little I'll go back down and see what I can do."

While waiting for the diver to go down again Cliff went into his stateroom and returned with a coil of slender but very strong nylon rope.

Lori glanced up at the fishing boat, catching her breath sharply.

"Dad!" she whispered, "those men are watching us through binoculars!"

He looked up quickly, ignoring his own admonition to pay no attention to them. He saw that Lori was right. Kelly and Nickerson both had binoculars and were studying every move that was made aboard the houseboat.

"Do—do you suppose they know that Mr. Mc-Millan found something on his last dive, Dad?"

"You bet they know it. There's no use in our trying to be secretive any more. They're watching everything that we do."

Nevertheless, when Frank was ready to go down again he went around to the other side of the *Betty Jo* and lowered himself hurriedly into the water, the nylon line securely tied about his waist. The outboard motor on the rival boat started up suddenly, and the sturdy fishing craft made a wide semicircle to a vantage point where they could see what was going on aboard the houseboat.

"Those men make me *so* mad!" Sharon exploded. "I'd like to go over there and tip their boat over for them!"

"Now that wouldn't be very nice," Cliff said mildly.

"What they're doing isn't very nice, either," she countered.

Cliff gave her a serious look. "I can understand why you feel that way, Sharon. But the Bible doesn't tell us that we should pay everyone back for the mean things they do to us. We're supposed to be kind to them."

She sneered sarcastically. "I suppose you're going to give them half of that million dollars in gold when you get it."

"There *isn't* any million dollars in gold, Sharon."

She wanted to answer him hotly, letting him know that she didn't believe him when he talked that way, even if he was a Christian. But she did not. There was something about Mr. Adams that kept her from saying what she had in mind. He was friendly and easy to approach, but he commanded respect at the same time.

Cliff held the nylon line loosely in his hand, letting it out as Frank went deeper into the river. After five minutes he jerked sharply on the line.

"Give me a hand," Cliff said, his voice tense. "Frank's ready for us to lift whatever he's tied onto the other end."

Captain Ellis and Rusty grasped hold of the rope and heaved their strength against it. The heavy object began to move slowly toward the surface. The muscles on the mens' arms bulged and their faces reddened as they strained against the rope.

"Want us to help?" Lori asked, moving forward uncertainly.

Her dad shook his head. "We'll get it!"

After a time they stopped to rest. "Whatever we're hooked onto, it's sure heavy," Captain Ellis murmured. "I can tell you that much."

"I was just thinking the same thing myself." Cliff grinned. "I'm beginning to wonder whether he hooked onto the *Margaret L.*"

"Or one of those boxes of gold," Rusty added, grinning mischievously, and breathing deeply.

"We'd better get with it," the *Betty Jo*'s skipper retorted, "or we never will find out what we've located."

Again they began to haul on the line in unison. Frank McMillan's head popped out of the water and an instant later they could make out the strange shape of a big, iron object, badly encrusted with rust.

"What is it?" Rusty demanded.

"Don't tell me that you've never seen a plow before!" Sharon answered scornfully.

They had found an old plow! It was the kind that was used on every farm before the invention and widespread use of the tractor.

Once the plow was at the surface of the water, its weight seemed to increase a great deal. The men pulled as hard as they could on the rope but could not move it more than an inch or two.

"I'm afraid we're going to need the help of you girls after all," Cliff said. "Come and give us a hand."

With their efforts added to those of the men, they managed to lift the plow onto the deck of the houseboat.

Mr. McMillan, who had just crawled out of the water, looked down at it. "That doesn't seem like much for all that effort," he said.

Cliff did not reply.

"The plow isn't much," Captain Ellis observed, "but at least we do know that we're on the right track. We must have located the old riverboat."

The archeologist did not answer him immediately. He chipped a bit of rust off the handle of the plow, thoughtfully. "Maybe," he said softly, "and maybe not."

Captain Ellis stared at him. "And just what do you mean by that?"

Cliff frowned. "I don't remember that there were any plows on the manifest. I want to check before I decide whether we've located the *Margaret L* or not."

He went into the stateroom and came back moments later. His angular face was solemn and his shoulders seemed to sag perceptibly.

"How about it?" Ellis spoke up. "Was she carrying any plows?"

Cliff's eyes gave the answer, even before he spoke. "I'm sorry," he mumbled. "But there were no plows aboard the *Margaret L*. They didn't even carry any plowshares."

Captain Ellis sighed deeply. "That's tough. For a while I thought maybe we'd hit her."

"So did I. The location was almost exactly right and the depthometer registered a shallow area, indicating there's something on the bottom below us." He turned to look across the river in the direction of the open fishing boat that was hovering off the port bow fifty yards away. "I guess there's nothing for us to do except to start over."

"I can tell you this much," Mr. McMillan broke in, "It's not going to be easy to find anything in water as muddy as this."

Cliff turned to the captain. "I think we might as well move over another twenty five yards and start looking again."

"How do we know that the manifest is right?" Rusty asked. "Couldn't there have been a mistake in it?"

" I suppose there could be, but it isn't likely." He wiped the sweat from his forehead. "Im convinced in my own mind that finding this plow means that we haven't located the *Margaret L* yet."

They continued their slow, methodical sweep of the river. The rest of the day dragged by without incident. Once or twice they stopped and anchored so Mr. McMillan could dive for a closer look, but they came across nothing that seemed to warrant a second dive in the same area. When night came the *Betty Jo* wearily made her way back to the dock.

"I don't know about you, Cliff," Captain Ellis said

at the dinner table that evening, "but I'm getting awfully discouraged."

"You shouldn't let it get you down." The archeologist managed a wan smile. "We've got some problems, but we've got as good a chance as anyone to find the old riverboat."

"I don't know about that. The boat's been lost for better than a hundred years and a lot of good rivermen have tried to locate her without success. That's one thing that's against us. Then too we've got Kelly and Nickerson out there shadowing every move. If we should find the *Margaret L* the chances are that they'd beat us to raising her."

"We can't quit yet," Mr. Adams answered.

Captain Ellis shrugged. "Staying out here all summer is OK with me. You're paying us for the houseboat by the week, so it's nothing to us one way or the other. But I hate to see anyone waste money, even when it benefits me."

Cliff made a half-hearted reply because he too was fighting a deep, growing depression. It looked as though everything he did, or tried to do, came out wrong.

Conversation at the dinner table that evening was almost nonexistent. As soon as the girls and Rusty had finished the dishes and cleaned the galley, they excused themselves and went to their rooms.

"I'm with Captain Ellis," Sharon said, making no attempt to mask her own disappointment. "I don't

think we're ever going to locate the riverboat and
raise her."

Lori did not answer.

"Look how long we've been working," her friend
continued, "and we haven't found one good solid
clue yet."

"We will," Lori said with determination. "I don't
know how or when, but we'll find her. And we'll
raise her too. Just wait and see."

Sharon sat down and kicked off her shoes. "I hope
you're right."

Lori finished her Bible reading alone in their
stateroom, knelt for prayer, and finally got into bed.
There had to be some reason, some *good* reason,
why none of the other searchers had found the
sunken riverboat; and why they hadn't found it
themselves. She knew all of the arguments the old
rivermen gave for the fact that the *Margaret L*
remained unfound.

They talked about shifting currents and ever
moving mud and sand that could pack in around an
object and hide it from view. They talked about
other boats that had gone down, never to be located
again. They talked of people who had drowned and
their bodies had never been given up by the muddy
Missouri River.

There *had* to be an answer somewhere! She sat
upright in bed, staring ahead in the darkness. But
where? That was the question that plagued her.

10

Amos Jefferson's Clue

Time seemed to stand still for Lori as she remained motionless on her bunk, eyes fixed on the darkened wall before her. There had to be something in all of this that they had missed—something everyone else who had tried to find the *Margaret L* had missed, as well. A riverboat so large couldn't simply vanish without a trace, regardless of what the old rivermen said.

She swung her feet over the side of the bed. Amos Jefferson probably knew more about this particular stretch of the Missouri than anyone else in the whole area. They should have asked him more about it while they were down there.

Lori got to her feet and walked silently to the big window, where she stood looking out into the impenetrable blackness of the night.

Amos had said something the other day that had sounded strange. She noticed it at the time and would have asked him about it but she thought he might be offended so she didn't. She hadn't thought of it since. Actually, she couldn't quite bring the statement back to mind, although it still bothered her.

"Sharon?" She spoke softly. "Sharon."

No answer.

"Sharon!"

Her friend stirred sleepily and mumbled something.

Lori called her name once more.

"What's the matter? What's wrong?" She sat up quickly.

"What did Amos Jefferson say to us when we were down there?"

"What did he *say* to us?" she echoed. "How would I remember that? He said lots of things."

"I know, but there was one thing he said that was sort of strange. What was it?"

"How would I know? Go back to sleep." With that she rolled over on her side.

"I'm sorry." Lori tried to think of what the old riverman had said that sounded so strange to her, but it remained just beyond the grasping fingers of her mind. At last she went back to bed and tried to sleep, but the matter still tormented her. When she got up the next morning she was still thinking about it. "You know, Sharon, I'd like to get Rusty to take us up to see Amos Jefferson again this morning, if Dad and Captain Ellis will let us."

"Why don't you wait until the middle of the night so you can wake him up and ask him what he said to

us, like you did me." She sounded grouchy, but Lori
knew that she didn't mean it.

"That sounds like an excellent idea."

"On second thought, maybe we'd better go in the
daytime. He might get out his shotgun and start
shooting at us if we wake him up in the middle of the
night the way you did me."

Rusty was eager to take the girls up to the old
tugboat. "At least it'll give us something to do for a
few hours. It won't be quite as boring as the last
week has been."

They got permission from Captain Ellis and Lori's
dad and set out, fighting the powerful current on
their way upstream. All the while Lori tried to
remember what the white haired old riverman had
said. It had something to do with the *Wren*, his old
tugboat, and it seemed as though it had something to
do with their son who had been lost in a storm.

"But I still can't remember what it was that he said
that bothered me so much," she exclaimed in
disgust.

"Don't look at me," Rusty told her. "I haven't got
the slightest clue what you're talking about. And for
that matter I can't see how Amos Jefferson could
possibly have told us anything that would help in
locating the *Margaret L.* After all, the old riverboat
went down more than a hundred years ago and I
don't suppose Amos is over eighty or eighty-five. We
know he's not a hundred."

"Now you're making fun of me."

He grinned at her good naturedly. "We wouldn't do *that*, would we, Sharon?"

The old man was on the tugboat when they got there. He must have seen them from some distance downstream. He was on deck, waving to them as they headed into the riverbank. He was glad to see them and talked to them for a minute. Then Lori brought up the purpose of their trip upriver to visit with him.

"Mr. Jefferson, would you tell us the story of the big flood again?" she asked.

Amos' eyes narrowed. "Why do you want to hear about that again?" he asked suspiciously.

Lori squirmed uncomfortably. "I don't know for sure. But there was something you said that— that—" She swallowed hard.

"That *what*?"

"I can't remember for sure, but something you said has been bothering me, that's all."

"Something I said?" Amos asked. Flattered to have such a responsive audience, the old man began his tale again. The three kids waited patiently as he repeated and embellished each detail. At last he came to the conclusion. "So, like I told you th' other day, I tied her up at the dock at the foot of Main Street and went into town to find the sheriff. He—"

Lori suddenly remembered what bothered her and she interrupted. "Amos, the town of Grenville is a mile away from the river. How could you have docked at Main Street?"

"It wasn't a mile away *then*, girl." He sounded as if he were explaining something to a small child. "That flood and ones before and ones after *all* changed the big river some."

"Well, thanks, Amos," Rusty joined in. "We've got to get back to the boat. It's time to start fixing supper."

They said their good-byes and soon they were in the dinghy heading back to the houseboat. Lori kept thinking hard about what Amos had said. Then, like turning the next page in a book, the answer stared her right in the face.

"That's it!" she shouted. "That's it!"

She startled Rusty so badly he cut the throttle to idling speed. "What are you talking about?"

"I just remembered what Amos said that bothered me. It'll help Dad find the *Margaret L*!"

He shook his head incredulously. "You must be kidding."

"Do you remember hearing him say that he raced to the dock at the foot of Main Street in Grenville, near where we're docked now with the *Betty Jo*?"

"I guess so." He shrugged his shoulders and accelerated the speed again. "But I don't see what that tells us about where the *Margaret L* is."

Lori leaned forward. "How far away from the foot of Main Street are we now?"

Rusty thought for a moment. "A mile or so, I guess."

"Doesn't that tell you something about the river at the time the *Margaret L* was sunk?"

Silence came over the little boat. Sharon pulled in a deep breath and expelled the air slowly.

"Are you trying to tell us that the river was in a different place than it is now?"

"Right! Haven't you read about the Missouri and how it has changed channels during floods? The river used to be near the town. It must have been over there when the riverboat went down."

Rusty thought about that for a moment. "If that's true, the riverboat isn't in the water at all. It's below the land!"

"Of course! Can't we go any faster Rusty? I can't wait to tell this to Dad!"

Cliff Adams listened intently as Lori and her companions told what they had learned. "What do you think, Captain?" he asked when they finished. "Does it sound logical to you?"

"The Missouri has had a history of changing channels. It's altogether possible."

The archeologist looked out across the water. "I'll have to make another trip to Lincoln to get an old map of this section of the river," he said. "And we'll have to have an electronic metal locater and some shovels." He paused to look at the other boat and smile broadly. "If this theory happens to be correct, there are going to be some very disappointed men out there."

Cliff left the *Betty Jo* as soon as it was dark,

driving off in his station wagon, taking Frank with him. Shortly after daylight they were back with the necessary equipment and the authorization to excavate on state owned ground.

"I've been doing a lot of thinking about this," he said. "If we're not careful, we're going to give ourselves away and have Kelly and his buddies tagging along behind, giving us trouble."

Captain Ellis nodded. "Of course, they don't have to know what's going on. McMillan and I can go out on the river and give them a good show while you and the kids try to locate the boat."

With the help of a surveyor's transit and the metal detector, Cliff and Rusty and the girls set to work. The first two days on land were almost exact duplicates of their earlier efforts on the river. Holding the metal detector a few inches from the ground they walked back and forth over the area that seemed the most likely to produce results. Every now and then the electronic device would indicate metal below the surface and they would dig frantically, uncovering an old horseshoe, an ax head or part of a shovel.

"We're in river sand," Cliff said, "so we must be on target as far as the old channel is concerned."

"But we still haven't found a trace of the *Margaret L*," Rusty observed.

"That's right." There was a faraway look in his eyes. "And, to tell you the truth, I'm beginning to wonder if we're *ever* going to find the old riverboat."

"Don't say that, Dad," Lori broke in. "We've *got* to find it!" Even though she knew how much the Carstigan diary meant to her dad, she was anxious to prove to everyone that he hadn't lied about the gold.

That evening after dinner Captain Ellis voiced his concern about Kelly and Nickerson. "Those characters are getting restless. I don't think we're going to be able to hold them off much longer. I know they're beginning to wonder where the rest of you are keeping yourselves. You can expect them to get mighty nosy any time."

Cliff pushed back from the table and got to his feet. "I'm sure you're right."

"Is there anything we can do to keep them from knowing about our work on land?"

"We're taking all the precautions we can."

In their stateroom before going to bed Sharon spoke of the *Margaret L* again and of Cliff's concern about finding her before anyone else did.

"He wouldn't be so anxious about it if it wasn't for all that gold."

Lori's impatience rose. "How many times do I have to tell you that there *isn't* any gold?"

"I'll believe that when I see it!"

"It's the truth!" she exclaimed in exasperation.

11

Something More than Gold

Two weeks crawled by, and there was little more
to show for their effort. They continued to add to
their assortment of metal objects that they had dug
from the former riverbed, but there was nothing to
indicate that they were even close to the wreckage
of the old riverboat.

Lori didn't say anything to anyone else, but she
wondered if there was really a *Margaret L* at all.
Maybe someone had already found it, she reasoned,
and got all of the things of any value from it. It
seemed strange to her that her dad still seemed as
optimistic as he had been before they left home.

The day they made their discovery started out like
all the rest. Cliff and Rusty marked off the area the
girls were to cover and Lori and Sharon took turns
walking slowly over it with the metal detector held
close to the ground. The first half of the hot, humid
morning was fruitless and it was beginning to look as
though the entire day was going to end the same as
the others. Toward evening Lori was using the metal
detector when the device reacted violently—much

more violently than when they had found the smaller objects.

"Sharon! Dad! Look!" Her voice trembled with excitement.

The others dropped what they were doing and came running over to her.

"Did you ever see such a reaction on the detector, Mr. Adams?" Rusty asked.

Cliff was excited but also cautious. "No, I've never seen the needle react this way before. Still, it may be that we've only found another plow."

"We'll soon find out!" Rusty snatched up a shovel and went to work. "We'll soon find out!"

Cliff took the other shovel and helped the redhead dig. After the sod was removed, the digging in the fine river sand was easy. In half an hour Rusty's shovel clinked against something hard.

"Hey!" he cried, "I think we've found something!"

The others crowded around, staring into the hole. There *was* something down there. Lori could see a small stretch of rusted iron. "W-what is it, Rusty?"

"I—I don't know yet." He was panting heavily from the exertion. Sweat soaked through his shirt and ran down his cheeks.

"Here," Cliff said, "let me dig for a while."

"I've just about got it."

An instant later Rusty dropped his shovel and bent over the rusted object, scooping the sand away with his hands. "An anchor!" he cried.

"An anchor!" Lori echoed. "We've found it, Dad! We've found the *Margaret L!*"

But his expression did not reveal such exultation. "We've found an old anchor," he corrected. "It may or may *not* belong to the *Margaret L.*"

"But she went down right in this area," Lori protested.

"There may have been other boats that sank in the same part of the river, Lori. We've got to have more proof than this."

"But it *could* belong to the *Margaret L*, couldn't it?"

"Yes." He nodded thoughtfully. "It could belong to the *Margaret L.*"

"How are we going to find out for sure?" she asked at last.

Cliff Adams did not reply for almost a minute.

"We don't even know if there is a boat here," he said at last. "A lot of boats lose anchors."

"How will we find out?" Sharon asked.

"There's too much sand to move to try and do it by hand. I think we'll have to get a bulldozer and scoop away most of it—or at least enough to show us whether there is a boat here."

"And if we *do* find out that the *Margaret L* is here, what do we do then?" Rusty wanted to know.

"We'll use the bulldozer as much as possible and finish the rest of the job by hand."

Mr. Adams pushed his shovel into the ground to

leave it where they had been working, but the kids were still examining the old anchor.

An instant later Lori cried out suddenly, "Dad, look at this!"

"What is it?" He bent down beside her and the old anchor she was examining.

"There's a name or some initials or something on this anchor."

"Let me see!" Using a small hammer, Cliff knocked off the rust scales on the portion of anchor Lori had uncovered.

"Bostwick Boat Works, Hannibal, Missouri," he read the inscription aloud.

Lori groaned. "That doesn't tell us anything," she said unhappily.

"Oh, but it *does*! It tells us a great deal!" He straightened slowly. "The *Margaret L* was made by the Bostwick Boat Works of Hannibal, Missouri! This anchor has got to belong to her!"

The girls stared at him numbly. After looking so long for the old riverboat, it scarcely seemed possible that the search was over.

"What are we going to do now?" Lori asked, the excitement of the moment hushing her voice.

"Find the gold bullion, of course!" Sharon exclaimed.

"We'd better get some probing rods first and see if we can find the wreckage of the boat. Once we locate it, we'll have to outline her, if we can, and then get the bulldozer." He started toward the car. "Do you girls want to come along?"

Lori glanced at her friend. "If you don't need us here."

"Rusty can look after things on this end, in case someone should wander out here and start digging on their own."

"Like Kelly and Nickerson?" the boy asked, trying to hide his concern.

"Don't worry about them," Cliff said, laughing. "They're still diving."

In two hours Cliff and the girls were back with the probing rods and they set to work. Lori and Sharon had supposed that using the rods would be a job of only an hour or two and that they would be ready for the bulldozer the following morning at the latest. But such was not the case.

They used the rods carefully, going over the ground with considerable care. It was two days before they actually located anything that could be the *Margaret L*, and another week before they had outlined the length and breadth of the buried boat. As the form of the wrecked riverboat began to take shape in the probing rods, Cliff Adams became more convinced than ever that they had found the *Margaret L*. The dimensions matched hers perfectly as far as they had gone.

"There's no doubt that we've found her," he said one evening.

"Aren't we about ready for the bulldozer, Dad?" Lori wanted to know.

He glanced at her. "Yes, Lori, I think we are."

Getting the bulldozer was only the matter of about an hour. Shortly after noon the following day the cumbersome earthmover rumbled onto the site and set to work under Cliff Adams' careful direction.

A few days' work with the bulldozer would be enough to expose the object completely. That would allow them to start the more painstaking work with shovels and wheelbarrows.

By the end of the second day the superstructure and a portion of the deck and the sides were freed from sand. By the end of the fourth day they were practically finished.

"How much longer will it take, Dad?"

"I'm not sure," he said, frowning. "But we ought to be through with the bulldozer by noon tomorrow."

"Come on," Rusty said, starting for the car. "It's getting dark and I'm about starved."

Lori hung back. "Do you think we ought to go away and leave the boat exposed like this?" she asked. "Aren't you afraid someone will steal something?"

"Nobody except the bulldozer operator knows what we've found and I got a promise from him not to say anything to anyone about it." Cliff opened the car door on the driver's side. "I don't think we've got anything to worry about."

Sharon eyed him curiously. "What if there is gold in the safe?" she asked.

"That's the least of my worries." He was still chuckling as they drove back toward the *Betty Jo*.

Before dawn the following morning, Cliff knocked on the door to the girls' stateroom. "Come on, Lori and Sharon. Let's get with it. We've got a lot of work to do today."

Sleepily they got up and dressed. "What do you suppose your dad wants us to do so early in the morning?" Sharon mumbled.

"He probably wants an early start on the excavating," Lori answered, yawning and stretching.

"The bulldozer won't be starting this early, will it?" Sharon wanted to know.

They left the houseboat as soon as they had breakfast, and drove back to the site where they had found the buried *Margaret L.*

"I suppose it seems strange getting you three kids up so early," Cliff told them apologetically, "but I thought we could get a couple of hours' work done by shovel before the bulldozer goes at it. He laughed good-naturedly. "Besides, I was so excited I wasn't able to sleep and I figured you couldn't either."

"It really didn't bother me that much," Sharon said.

He parked the car a hundred yards from the excavation and they walked toward it, their shovels in their hands. Dawn was just creeping over the eastern horizon stealthily, pushing the darkness aside. They could just make out the depression in the sand and the high piles on either side.

"I'll be glad when this is over," Sharon said, shivering.

"You aren't scared, are you?" Rusty asked. "I didn't think a girl like you would be scared."

Her cheeks flushed. "I'm not, really. I'll just feel better when this is over."

"So will I," Lori added.

Cliff Adams, who was a step or two ahead of his young companions, paused on the rim of the excavation, staring straight down. There was something definitely different about the exposed portion of the *Margaret L.* "Rusty," he said, turning slightly. "Is that the way we left it?"

The boy frowned. "I didn't think we had exposed that much of the superstructure," he said. "And I know we didn't take any sand from the inside."

Lori looked at Mr. Adams. "Somebody came to the old boat after all, and started to work on it!" Her pulse quickened.

"That's right! We didn't touch a shovel after the bulldozer finished last night." He dashed forward. "Somebody has been here trying to help himself!"

On the deck the foursome stopped, staring into the cabin. Someone had indeed been working, probably most of the night. Much of the sand had been carried out of the cabin.

"Do you suppose anything has been taken?" Lori whispered fearfully.

Cliff switched on his flashlight to reveal an old safe in one corner of the cabin. "Those stories about the gold! he exclaimed. "I might have known!"

At that instant Buford Kelly stepped up behind them, a shotgun held carelessly in his hands.

"All right!" he snarled. "That's far enough! All of you! Stay right where you are!"

"You'll never get away with this, Kelly," Cliff told him. "You know that, don't you?"

"I'll take my chances."

"What are you looking for? The gold that's supposed to be aboard?"

"The gold that *is* aboard," Kelly corrected him. "It was thoughtful of you to locate this old riverboat for us. We might not have been able to find her if it hadn't been for you."

"Just don't destroy any of the items of historical value," Cliff said. "That's all I ask."

"That's enough talk for now. Come on! Get back out of the way so we can blow the door on that safe."

Cliff winced. That could ruin everything if they used a charge that was too large. "Did you try to open it by working the combination?"

"Don't be funny!"

While Kelly held the little group at shotgun point some distance from the *Margaret L*, Nickerson put the explosive in place and touched it off. The noise echoed through the still morning air, and acrid white smoke poured out of the cabin.

Nickerson sped into the smoke-filled cabin. "We did it!" he cried. "We did it!"

"What about the gold?" Kelly shouted.

"It's all here! Every little pouch of it!" They heard him faintly.

With that, Kelly forgot his captives and turned to the cabin. Cliff and Rusty both jumped on him so suddenly he thudded to the ground.

"What's going on out there?" Nickerson demanded, coming to the cabin door, a leather pouch in each hand.

"All right," Cliff warned. "Don't move! *I've* got the shotgun now!"

"We were just joking," Kelly protested. "We didn't plan on taking your gold or—or anything else. We—" His voice trailed away.

"You're wasting time telling that to us. Save it for the sheriff."

"You—you aren't going to have us arrested, are you?"

"You're a mind reader, Kelly. We certainly are."

"But—But—"

"Go over and get one of those pouches from Nickerson, Rusty. Let's have a look in it."

"What did I tell you?" Sharon said smugly to no one in particular. "I *knew* you were after the gold." She faced Lori. "You couldn't trick me with all that talk about a Christian refusing to lie."

Rusty took the pouch from Tim Nickerson and poured the contents into his hand. He groaned audibly.

"What's wrong?"

"Pebbles!" he exclaimed. "Nothing but pebbles!" He shook the leather pouch as though something of value must have stayed inside.

"That's about what I thought," Cliff said. "I was sure there was no gold aboard the *Margaret L.*"

Rusty studied his face seriously. "Why would anyone go to the trouble to fill those pouches with pebbles?"

"Pebbles," Kelly muttered in disgust. "All of this trouble for a few little stones."

"They're not just pebbles. They're ore samples. They were probably being taken somewhere to be assayed. That's probably how the rumor started about the gold. I'm sure the manifest should have included that," Mr. Adams explained.

"Ore samples!" Kelly spat the words out.

Cliff handed Rusty the shotgun and hurried to the safe. Lori had already begun scooping out the debris.

She held up part of an old Mason jar.

"It's broken, Dad. The old jar was broken in the explosion!"

"What about the diary? Is it all right?"

She picked up the old sheets of paper from among the broken bits of glass.

"The events in the life of Esau Carstigan," she read.

"That's it!" he shouted triumphantly. "We've found what we came after!"

"Some sheets of paper?" Nickerson exclaimed.

"You didn't find *your* gold," Cliff told him, laughing, "but I found *mine*! I got exactly what I was looking for."

When Cliff and Rusty finally drove away with their two captives, Sharon turned to Lori. "Your dad wasn't looking for gold, after all."

"That's what I've been trying to tell you," Lori said, smiling.

She pulled in a deep breath. "I thought you were just protecting him when you said that he wouldn't lie because he's a Christian. I guess I didn't believe that being a Christian made a person be honest."

Sharon hesitated and Lori said nothing.

"Lori," Sharon said again, her voice quiet.

"Yes?"

"Do you suppose God could make *me* a Christian like you and your dad are?"

"I *know* He can!"

"Would you tell me again what you said before about becoming God's child?"

With a silent prayer for help, Lori shared with her friend the way to know God personally. After they prayed, Sharon said, "Lori, I've discovered something better than a million dollars in gold."

Moody Press, a ministry of the Moody Bible Institute, is designed for education, evangelization and edification. If we may assist you in knowing more about Christ and the Christian life, please write us without obligation to: Moody Press, c/o MLM, Chicago, Illinois 60610.